THE PIPER

Matthew Ryan

THE WYGHT ISLAND CHRONICLES

BOOK 1

THE PIPER

***

MATTHEW RYAN

This edition first published in Great Britain in 2022 by Elite Island Publishing

Cover Design: Ambient Pixel Designs

1st Edition

ISBN: 9798361978748

Elite Island Publishing

Follow us on:

Dedicated to my wife,
Maria,
Always and Forever x

Matthew Ryan

CONTENTS

Matthew Ryan

The Piper

Into the street the Piper stept,
Smiling first a little smile,
As if he knew what magic slept
In his quiet Pipe the while.

- Robert Browning
The Pied Piper of Hamelin

Matthew Ryan

PROLOGUE

THE BLIND BOY

The scream that came from the mouth of the blind boy sounded inhuman. He clawed at a stone wall, with bloodied fingers and nails, trying to get in. The boy needed to find the cave so that he could be with the Piper.

The boy was one of over a hundred children who had followed the wonderful sound of music that came from the Piper's pipe. The children from the town of Hamelin had skipped merrily behind the strange man as he led them along. They were laughing and singing as they made their way to what the Piper had called "a cave of wonders."

The blind boy, however, had fallen behind the group. Initially, several of the children had taken turns holding his hand, but then a loose stone caused him to fall and no one came to his aid. The Piper and the children carried on merrily skipping and dancing toward the cave. The blind boy cried out, but no one paid him any attention.

The boy got to his feet and felt his way along trying to find the entrance to the wonderful cave. As he felt his way along, his fingers finally touched rock. He searched more, feeling with his hands. It was a rocky wall that he felt. No doubt the entrance to the cave was nearby and so he followed the wall, feeling the rocks and stones as he went.

The blind boy began to panic, he could not find the entrance. He could, however, hear the sound of children laughing coming from behind the wall. The boy shouted and pounded on the rocks but the noise faded away to nothing. All he could hear was the sound of his breathing. The boy tried to kick and pull on the rocks but nothing happened. He was beginning to feel more desperate and so tried to claw his way through the wall, but still, nothing would give.

As the men of the town approached, with their torches raised and their pitchforks in hand, they saw the horror on the boy's face. The boy was crying and bleeding as he pounded with his fists on the rocky wall. His knees were grazed and blood covered his fingers and hands.

As they carried him away he tried to escape. The boy screamed and cried out hysterically.

'Please, I want to be with the Piper! Let me go!'

The men never found the cave and the children were never seen again, but the people of Hamelin remembered the Piper's promise.

"I will return to exact vengeance on the wicked!"

PART 1

THE TOWN OF BRADING

Matthew Ryan

CHAPTER 1

THOMAS & OWEN

All Thomas had ever wanted was a place to finally call home. It occurred to Thomas, as he trudged along the muddy road, that this would be the seventh town he and his family had lived in during his short life of sixteen years. He hoped this town would be the one, but he seriously doubted it.

As Thomas walked with his family he brushed off some dried tomato seeds from his arm. The townsfolk of Havenstreet had given the family a send-off in the form of rotting vegetables and abusive shouting. He never did like that place and was glad to be gone.

Thomas did wonder though, what this new town would be like. Brading was a key town on the Wyght Island. It was close to the main port for ships and was famous for having the freshest water on the island. Best of all though, was that they had relatives there who had helped by finding a home for them, and work too.

The first thing Thomas noted, as he walked toward the entrance to the town, was the smell. His father, a tall lean man with greying hair and a short trimmed beard, led the way pushing a wheelbarrow.

'Pig swill, always flaming pig swill! For once it'd be nice to walk into a town and smell something different,' said Thomas' father.

Thomas laughed at his Pa, they had always had similar thoughts. Great minds think alike apparently, or was it simply the bond of a father and son? Such things were beyond him, but he would no doubt come to question that thought as time went by.

'Stop complaining Pa!' said Mary, his wife, and critic. 'If you had more money and more sense we wouldn't have to keep moving from pillar to post!'

'I know my dearest but times a' hard. Everyone's feeling the pinch. Maybe we'll settle down this time Ma.'

'Let's hope so!' she replied.

Thomas never understood why his parents spoke to each other using those names, Ma and Pa. Maybe his father called his wife Ma because it was short for Mary but he doubted it. Pa was definitely not short for his father's actual name which was Owen, but his mother and father's relationship had always struck him as odd. They were both so different and there never appeared to be any love or intimacy between the two. They just seemed to go through the motions of being married.

Thomas glanced at each of his siblings as the family moved on. He wanted to make sure they were still ok after the long walk. Being the eldest, Thomas felt more like a parent than a brother. Behind him was his sister Lucy who had not long ago become a woman. Thomas still didn't understand what that meant despite being her senior by three years and being still classed as a boy himself. Lucy was leading an old donkey pulling a small rickety cart that was laden down with goods. Thomas' other sibling was his younger brother John. He was asleep inside the wheelbarrow that Owen was pushing. He was nine years old and lame. Thomas felt a deep love for him and hated the thought of the hardships John would face as he grew older. Thomas truly loved his brother and sister and knew he would always be there for them despite his own choices in life, whatever they may be.

As the family neared the entrance to the town they saw the sign with its name, "Brading". Below the sign sat two rats who were grooming themselves, who paid the family no attention as they walked past. Brading looked no different from many of the other villages and towns Thomas had lived in before. Thomas could see houses of stone and timber that were no doubt owned by those better off financially. For those not as well off were the stone cottages with thatched roofs, and there were even a few hovels that could be seen for those that were poor.

The family walked past what appeared to be the village green that had a maypole in its centre that looked as if it hadn't been danced around for many, many years. They passed a small cemetery where everything was deathly quiet apart from a small cluster of rats scurrying around the headstones.

The street itself was very quiet except for a few chickens who were clucking and examining the floor looking for morsels to peck at. Thomas bent down and picked up a small stone and threw it at a lone cockerel who squawked in response. Mary immediately slapped Thomas around the back of his head.

'What are you doing boy? Do you want people to think we're vulgar?'

'I'm sorry mother. It's just so quiet here!'

'That it be lad,' chipped in his father. 'That it be.'

'Just mind your manners, Thomas. You're being a bad example to your brother and sister,' said his mother.

Thomas nodded and kept his head down as they continued walking along the stone street. As they walked they began to hear the sound of singing. The singing was coming from a church that Thomas saw was called "St Mary the Virgin".

'At least they're religious in this town Pa! Nowt good comes from those without God,' said Mary.

'Amen to that Ma!' replied Owen.

Matthew Ryan

As they neared the church its doors swung open and dozens of people began to stream out, chattering about the service and the signs of the times. There were men, women, and children all dressed in their church best. Those that were rich, or of higher class, stood out clearly and stayed in tight-knit groups away from the general members of the Congregation.

Many people passed by Thomas and his family as they walked. Some were casting curious looks at them while others ignored them completely, but the family pressed on keeping their heads down to avoid the look of judgement or disgust. Thomas wondered if the folk of Brading had heard the rumours from their last town. Rumours travelled fast apparently. Besides failing to pay their rent, Thomas' father had been blamed for the burning of the tavern there, an accusation that was never founded but sadly could not be shaken.

The family pressed on through the town and passed the town hall and also what appeared to be a small building that was being used as a school. The school had a small grassy area behind a picket fence where young Children could be seen playing under the watchful eye of a woman with a sturdy face and an even sturdier walking stick. The woman watched with suspicion as Thomas and his family trundled past heading further into town.

As they walked along the street they could see a tavern, a bakery, a tanner's, and a large stable. There were also several other small businesses that were common for a town such as this. Thomas could see various traders inside their shops working or selling their wares. The main road through the town was better kept than the one they had been travelling on, but it was still dirty with puddles in places.

After several turns and another hundred yards, the family finally arrived at their destination. It was a rundown cottage with what appeared to be an even more run-down stable next to it. Next to the front door was nailed a piece of wood with a name carved on it. It said: "Bugle Cottage".

The Piper

'We're here. This be the place, my love,' said Owen. 'It'll look like home in no time.'

'It's going to need a lot of work Pa!' replied Mary.

'True, but least we have somewhere to live.'

Thomas looked doubtfully at the cottage and opened his mouth to speak but then thought better of it. The last slap he had received still throbbed. He headed over to Lucy who had finally caught up with them with the donkey and the cart.

'You took your time!' he joked.

'Back off Thomas! I can only go as fast as the donkey!' she replied.

Thomas laughed.

'I'm only jesting with you. What do you think of the place?'

'It looks ok on the outside.'

'That's what the Christians thought of the Colosseum!'

They both laughed.

'Well let's hope it's better than that!' she said.

Thomas headed over to the wheelbarrow still laughing. His father had put it down and was talking with his mother. Thomas looked at the sleeping boy laying inside. He bent down and woke the boy up.

'Wakey, wakey John. You've been asleep for hours.'

The boy stirred and stifled a yawn.

'Are we there yet?' said the boy.

'Just arrived.'

'Is it as nice as Pa said it would be?'

'It looks ok from the outside, but we need to see it properly.'

Thomas reached down and lifted John out of the barrow. He then swung him around to his back in a fast, effortless manner. John then linked his arms around Thomas' neck as he was carried off.

'Come on trouble,' said Thomas smiling. 'Let's take a look at our new home.'

His father opened the door to the rundown cottage and the family walked in.

***

'Get out!' came the scream as the family entered the cottage.

Owen entered first and laughed out loud at what he saw. An old woman was hitting a kitchen unit with a straw brush. A rat had perched itself on top of it and she was trying to scare it away.

'Aunt Emmy!' called Owen. 'You look like you need help!'

The old woman turned around in surprise. She looked very old and frail but moved with the strength and energy of someone half her age and double her size.

'Owen! Weren't expecting you 'til later lad! Come in, come in!'

Owen walked over and embraced her.

'It's so good to see you, my boy. You look well. Your mother would have been so proud to see you with your family.'

'Thank you auntie and thank you for arranging somewhere for us to stay.'

He took the broom from her and began to usher the rat outside.

'You remember my wife, Mary?' he said.

'Of course. Lovely to see you again my dear. And these are the nippers no doubt?'

'Yes, aunt Emmy,' replied Mary. 'This is Thomas and Lucy. John is on Thomas' back.'

'The cripple! I'm so sorry my dearest,' said aunt Emmy to John. 'Better off dead they said of you when you were born. Trouble and strife for your whole life, but what do them there quacks know! You'll do well here my lad.'

She grinned a toothless grin at him causing him to squirm uneasily on Thomas' back.

'She means no harm John,' soothed Thomas.

'That's right my boy. I means no 'arm.'

She cackled and turned to Mary.

'How was your trip?'

'The weather held but the roads were wet and filthy. It shall take a month of Sundays to dry our shoes,' Mary complained.

'At least your here now my dear. Come, get your things in and I'll light a fire,' said aunt Emmy as she headed toward the fireplace.

The family sat around the fire that aunt Emmy had lit in the main room. There was the smell of charcoal and the crackling of wood in the room as the family huddled together. Wet clothes were hanging from various places surrounding the fire, and their shoes were lined up neatly in front of it. The family were each under blankets and sharing a large cup of warm milk, which was passed among them as they talked.

All listened to aunt Emmy as she was finishing her tale of how she once met a man with black skin with the bones of an animal through his nose and cheeks. All were enthralled by the story. As the tale finished Mary spoke up.

'So tell us about the town of Brading aunt Emmy. Anyone to keep an eye out for?'

'Brading be a good town, well-built and thriving. There be a number of unsavoury characters and the rats here I'm sure are breeding like rabbits, but overall it's fine. There's a few people to keep an eye on mind.'

'Like who auntie?' asked Owen.

'Well, firstly there's the Mayor, Lord Mulberry.'

'What's he like?' he asked.

'He's a mindless, bigoted, old fool. But long as ya pay ya taxes he'll leave you alone.'

'Sounds like every other Mayor we've encountered. Anyone else?' asked Owen.

'There's the priest, Reverend Nicholas.'

'You can't beat a good service. What's he like?' asked Mary.

'If his love of God was as great as his love for food and drink, he could rival Abraham himself,' aunt Emmy cackled.

The family laughed along with her.

'So he likes a drop of wine does he!' exclaimed Mary.

'Wine, mead, rum, whatever he can get 'is hands on. He also has a taste for other things a little sweeter and a little younger, but we'll not speak of such things in front of the nippers!'

Both Owen and Mary shook their heads in disgust.

'Another one to watch out for is Lady Barton,' aunt Emmy added. 'She lives in the big manor house on the hill. She be as rich as someone who just happened on the Kings family jewels'

'No husband?' asked Mary.

'No, no. Dead and buried.' aunt Emmy replied. 'Apparently Captain of the guard, back in the day.'

'What's she like?' asked Thomas.

'Too old for you, young shaper m'lad.'

The family burst into laughter while Thomas blushed.

'I didn't mean it like that!' he said defensively.

'Only playing my boy,' aunt Emmy laughed. 'She be the local money lender.

Nice enough when you're on her good side. Mind ya back with 'er though.'

'We'll remember that auntie,' said Owen.

'Everyone else ere be ok. Some are salt of the earth, others scum of the earth, Just let me know if you need anything. We ain't got much but we'll share what we ave.'

'Thank you, auntie,' said Owen and Mary in unison.

Aunt Emmy stood to leave and turned to Owen. 'Pop by the smithy in the morning and uncle will get you working. Bring Thomas and Lucy too.'

'Will do auntie, and thanks again,' he replied.

Owen showed her out of the door and sat back down with his family. For a few moments, Owen sat in front of the fire and reminisced on his past and his aunt and uncle.

After leaving the family home to find his own way on the island, Owen's parents became very sick. He returned five years later, with a pregnant wife in tow, to find that his parents were long dead. His parent's home and business were sold to pay off their debts and his aunt Emily and uncle Rupert were the last family he had. Aunt Emmy was his mother's sister and he viewed her just like a mother. Uncle Rupert was a nice guy, a hard worker. He had learned to be a blacksmith from Owen's father and had bought a stable in Brading and turned it into a smithy. He was getting very old and had no children so was excited to hear that Owen and his family wanted to come to live there.

Uncle Rupert and aunt Emily had rented the cottage so that Owen and his family could have somewhere to live. It was planned that Owen would inherit the smithy upon uncle Rupert's death and would try to build a family name in the smithy business. Until that time, however, Owen was to relearn the trade from his uncle. The same trade that Owen's father had taught him all those years ago.

'I've got a really good feeling about this Ma,' said Owen.

'Me too,' she replied. 'The place needs a bit of work but we'll soon make it a home.'

'Absolutely!' replied Owen.

<u>Matthew Ryan</u>

Owen noticed that the three children had all dozed off in front of the warm crackling fire. Owen got up from his chair and moved to a stack of chopped wood.

He picked up another log and put it on top of the others that were burning away in the fireplace.

'Let the nippers sleep,' he said. 'And let's start unpacking. We've got a lot of sorting to do to make it more homely.'

'Good idea Pa,' replied Mary. 'Let's get to work.'

The two left the room without disturbing the children and began to unpack and put the cottage in order.

CHAPTER 2

MARY & THOMAS

Mary was nervous. Over the past few days, she and the family had kept their heads down and interacted little with those in the town. Her husband Owen had begun to work at the smithy with his uncle Rupert, and Thomas and Lucy joined when extra work was available. The reason she was nervous was that they were heading to church. This would be the first time as a family that they would interact properly with the community since their arrival, and they were all apprehensive. She was especially apprehensive not only because of meeting the others that lived in Brading but also because of the service itself.

Mary had a very strong belief in God and the good book, but she was finding that not only were the priests hypocrites but also that they taught things of their own design. This greatly distressed Mary, but she tried to control her feelings in this regard. And so she got ready and helped her family to get ready too. They dressed well that Sunday morning. Owen, Thomas, and John wore their best jackets and even cleaned their shoes. Mary and Lucy wore their best dresses and tied ribbons in their hair.

The Smith family headed out wondering what the priest and the townsfolk would be like. They trudged up the street toward the church trying to avoid not only the puddles but also the rats too.

'Flaming things!' cried Owen, as a rat scurried over his foot.

'They're a nuisance pa,' said Lucy. 'I had to chase one out of my bed yesterday.'

'Did you hear that Ma!'

'I heard Pa. Disgusting, filthy things,' replied Mary.

They continued on and heard the bells begin to ring from the church steeple.

'Everyone looking forward to the service?' Mary asked.

The three children nodded unenthusiastically.

'I'm looking forward to it Ma. It'll be nice to hear a fresh set of vocals declaring the good news of our Lord,' said Owen.

As they neared the church they saw many families heading there too. Some gave customary nods while others refused to even give eye contact. The family headed up the steps and walked into the large nave. There were dozens of people milling about talking and finding seats. Mary noticed that the three children were uncomfortable. They were keeping their heads down and talking quietly among themselves. No doubt they were a little overwhelmed by being there but she knew it was for their own good. Aunt Emmy and Uncle Rupert were waiting for them and helped them to find seats along the cold bare wood of one of the nearby pews.

The reverend, an obese man in his sixties, mounted the pulpit, and everyone hushed and took their seats. The pulpit creaked under the weight of the reverend's large girth. He then began to give the sermon.

After an hour of the reverend giving warnings about the anti-Christ, and how each of them is a sinner and deserves to burn in the fires of hell, the family followed the crowd out of the church. Mary was a little shocked by the service the reverend had given. The service itself was a little doom and gloom, but the message appeared sound. The thing that shocked her most though was the priest himself. Reverend Nicholas was one of the most grotesque people she had ever seen. He was obese in size and his loud booming voice grated her. He was physically unclean and she did not doubt that he was morally unclean too. He was a man she would not want her family, or even herself, to spend any time with. She vowed to try to keep contact with him to a very minimum.

As they began down the steps of the church to head home the reverend Nicholas caught up with them, pushing his large form through the crowd.

'It was lovely to see you all at church today my friends,' began the reverend. 'Too many are forgetting about our Lord and the wonderful work he does. I hope you enjoyed the service.'

'Yes, it was very instructive reverend,' replied Owen. 'Let me introduce my family. This is my wife Mary. And these are my children Thomas, Lucy, and John.'

The children all said hello in unison.

'It's very nice to meet you reverend,' said Mary over-enthusiastically. 'The service was a powerful one. The interloper is certainly among us today.'

'That he is my dear,' replied the vicar. 'He watches from the shadows and draws each sinner headlong into his own sin. We must be ever watchful.'

'Amen to that!' said Owen.

The reverend put his hand on Lucy's head. 'Such a lovely child. Sweet as a peach,' he said admirably. 'I look forward to getting to know her, and you all, a little better.'

This statement made Mary feel very uncomfortable. She felt her heart thumping in her chest and she began to clench her hands into fists. She saw Owen look at her with concern on his face.

'Thank you reverend,' said Owen. 'Also, thank you for your time and the service but we must be going,'

Owen began to usher his family down the steps of the church.

'Have a good day my friends.'

The vicar then turned and began speaking to others in his vicinity.

The family walked quickly away from the church and headed home via the town square.

They passed others who were also heading away from the church. These greeted the Smith family, but they also looked eager to be getting home too. As the family walked they were suddenly intercepted by a tall slim fellow in his sixties. The man wore a bright red coat with a gold chain hanging from around his neck. The man also wore a tall black hat that made him appear even taller than he actually was.

'Good morning,' said the man. 'I'm Lord Mulberry. I am the Mayor of Brading. It was lovely to see you all at church today.'

'It's good to meet you my Lord.' replied Owen.

Owen bowed low, as did Thomas who was carrying John. Mary and Lucy curtsied.

'Have you settled in?' asked the Mayor.

'Yes my Lord,' Owen replied. 'It's a lovely town.'

'It certainly is!' I hear you are a blacksmith and your lady wife is very good at needlework.'

'That's right, my Lord' replied Owen.

'Good, good. I may have some work for you both on my estate.'

'That's very nice of you, my Lord,' said Mary.

'I'll pop by your home later this afternoon to discuss it with you,' said the Mayor. 'I believe you're living at the Bugle cottage. Is that correct?'

'Yes my Lord. We'd be happy to see you and help with whatever needs doing,' said Owen.

'Until then. Good day to you,' said the Mayor.

'And to you my Lord,' said Mary as she curtsied and Owen bowed.

The family headed off as the Mayor bowed his head to them and also left.

As they turned the corner, Mary turned to Owen.

'What do you think he wants of us Pa?'

'I don't know Ma. The money will help though and at least we'll be in his good books.'

'True, but we better make sure we do a good job. The last thing we want is to get on the wrong side of him.'

'Very true Ma.

'I think we better have another tidy of the house before he comes and tidy up the stable too. It'll be good to have the place looking nice. We'll look more respectable.'

'We are respectable Ma,' said Owen.

'I know Pa, but people do judge on appearances.'

'That be true, we'll start working on it as soon as we're back,' he replied.

At that, the family continued on and headed home.

***

It had been about an hour after arriving back from the church service that Thomas, Lucy, and John, were told to make themselves scarce. They had all helped tidy the house ready for the visit by the Mayor but their parents didn't want them there. Lucy took John in his barrow down to the nearby docks, known as "The Havens". She wanted to see if she could scrounge a few coins off the sailors. The sight of a crippled boy might open their purses, or so she believed. Thomas on the other hand wanted to have a wander around Brading. His uncle Rupert had said that he may need to do deliveries now and then, and so needed to know the layout of the town.

His journey began from home and he walked West toward the smithy. It was a journey that took about ten minutes but was fairly straightforward. On route, he passed the town square with its cluster of businesses. The town Market House was located there with the famed bull ring outside. In the middle of the square was a signpost. The signpost gave arrows. North said Upper Ryde, East said The Havens, South said Sandown, and West said, Newport. Thomas followed the arrow North. He wanted to start at the beginning of town to see what each building and road was called.

The streets were fairly quiet. It was Sunday afternoon and the shops and stalls were all closed. Some of the townsfolk were seen wandering about, but most would have been at home. As Thomas walked down the main street of the town, he saw a middle-aged man who was sweeping a patch of road outside the tavern. The man saw him and called out.

'Good afternoon young man. You're one of the Smiths!'

It wasn't a question but Thomas replied regardless and approached the man.

'Yes, my name is Thomas. Good afternoon sir.'

'I like you already. No one ever calls me sir!'

Thomas laughed.

'My name is Charlie Cooper,' said the man. 'I'm the landlord of the good old Kyngs Arms here!'

He pointed proudly to the tavern door behind him.

'Wow, it must be great owning a tavern!' Thomas said.

'It certainly can be a hoot. You don't happen to be looking for a job do you lad? I could do with a young pair of hands to help with the barrels.'

'Unfortunately not. I'm going to be working at the Smithy with my Pa and Uncle.'

'That's a shame. The serving girls are great but not strong enough to help with the heavy lifting. The barrels can be a particular pain to lift on your own!'

'I'm sorry. It does sound good though!' Thomas said.

'Let me know if you change your mind.'

'Thank you, Mr Cooper.'

At that, Mr Cooper carried on sweeping leaving Thomas to his task.

Thomas continued on, mentally noting which shops were where and the names of the various roads. He passed a few of the folk whom he recognised from church who greeted him. It was as he finished his walk on the main road that he felt something strange. He felt as if someone was watching him. He turned around to look but didn't see anything out of the ordinary. There were a few folks walking about and Mr Cooper was still sweeping, but no one was paying any attention to him.

It's just my imagination, Thomas thought to himself as he carried on walking.

Thomas headed off again walking back up the main road and heading south. He walked passed the town square again and also the signpost in the centre of town. He continued on the main road but again he began to feel uneasy. He looked around, but all he saw was a rat running along behind him. Thomas stopped walking and waited. The rat carried on running up toward him, and then past him, paying him no attention.

I'm just jumping at shadows, he thought to himself and smiled.

He carried on and turned West up a road named "The Mall" that led back toward the smithy. The Mall was a road that had fewer builders but notably had two farms located on it and a big manor house up a dirt track.

He walked along the road but had that strange feeling again. Someone was definitely watching him, maybe even following him. He quickly turned and saw a figure in a red cloak duck behind a bush about twenty yards away.

'Hello!' called Thomas. 'Is someone there?'

There was no reply.

Thomas walked back toward the bush expecting someone or something to jump out at him. He approached the bush and peered through the leaves and branches, but he saw nothing. He walked around the bush, but again nothing was there. He looked about perplexed. He was absolutely sure that he saw someone there. It was someone in a red cloak.

Feeling more uneasy, Thomas walked off again but headed home. He didn't like the thought of being watched any longer.

CHAPTER 3

LUCY & JOHN

Lucy had been given a straight choice, work in the smithy with Thomas or go to school with John. To Lucy it was simple, she would rather work at the smithy. If the so-called school was actually going to teach her anything then she would have jumped at the chance, but she knew it would be the same as any other she'd been to. It would be a case of a mistress or master simply watching over them and keeping them out of trouble. True, she may hear stories of different times and distant places, but she assumed from the look of the schoolmistress that the woman had probably never left the island, maybe not even left the town from the way she carried herself. So Lucy chose to work.

The smithy was much like any other that she had seen in her short life. It was a bustle of smoke, noise, and sweat. Her father and uncle Rupert were busy forging tools inside the main building, and Lucy was told to simply stack the wood in the yard that her brother Thomas was chopping.

It was late morning and a gloriously sunny day. Thomas had built up a sweat and was chopping the wood topless. Lucy had stacked a good amount of wood at this point and they had both made good progress, so decided to stop for a quick water break. Thomas sat on the chopping block wiping the sweat from his brow with his discarded top, while Lucy sat nearby on a stack of wood sipping water from a metal flagon.

'What do you think of the town?' asked Thomas.

'I'm still deciding.' she replied. 'We've only been here about a week, but it does seem better than that last place we were at!'

'That's true. It's good to be near the river though. The water here is a lot fresher to drink,' said Thomas as he drank deeply from his own flagon.

'What did you make of the service yesterday?' asked Lucy.

'It was good, but the priest was a bit of a beast! I think I was more focussed on him than on the message.'

'He was truly vile,' laughed Lucy.

Thomas laughed too.

'How have you been coping with the change?' he asked. 'I know it gets you down us having to keep moving.'

'I'm fine, but it is frustrating though!'

'You know Pa, if there's any such thing as bad luck then he's the one that'll find it!'

'I know, but sometimes it seems as if he looks for trouble.'

'It's the drink,' said Thomas 'That brown stuff rots his brain. That's why I'm never going to drink it!'

'You've had it before though.'

'True but I had just turned fourteen and trust me, now I've had it, I don't want it again! It's horrid stuff!'

Lucy laughed.

'Do you think this time we'll call this place home?' she asked.

'I hope so! I mean it's the family business this time and he's promised Ma that he'll stop the drinking. Maybe this time it really will be home.'

'I do hope so. It'll be nice to settle down as a family properly.'

'I know, but regardless you, me and John have each other and we'll get through it together.'

'Thanks, Thomas,' she said kindly.

'Come on little Sis, back to work. We don't want the old man breathing down our necks!'

'No way!' she laughed.

The two got up and began chopping and stacking the wood again.

After several hours of hard graft, Thomas and Lucy had finished chopping and stacking the wood. Thomas had to stay at the smithy to do some extra work but Lucy was allowed to go, and so she skipped her merry way out of the yard heading toward home. It was on her short journey that she saw the river Yar. The river looked beautiful with the sun reflecting off the clear blue water. Lucy decided to head down to take a closer look.

As she approached she saw that it was even more lovely than she first thought. The river was surrounded by colourful, elegant flowers on both banks. There were ducks and geese nestled in the shade of one of the great oaks nearby and a rabbit with a litter could be seen on one of the nearby banks. The scene was picturesque. Lucy walked down the bank toward the water and sat on a large stone. She took off her shoes and socks and dipped her feet into the cool refreshing water. She spread her toes and slowly kicked at the slow-moving currents. She looked about and not a soul could be seen. There were bridges about a hundred yards away North and South of her and beyond the bridge to the South was the town's water mill. She could see the wheel of the mill, turning slowly. In the middle of the river, Lucy saw what appeared to be a small island. It was covered in five-foot high bushes and had a young tree growing from the middle of it.

One day I'll explore that island, she thought to herself. *It'll be a nice place to be alone with my thoughts.*

She continued to sit for another ten minutes or so feeling the sun on her face and the water between her toes before she decided to make a move and head home. She picked up her shoes and socks and began to put them on. The task was made more difficult by her now wet feet.

As Lucy was tying her last lace, she looked and noticed something strange. The rabbits were gone but not just them, but also the ducks and geese as well. Normally this wouldn't have struck Lucy as odd, but they hadn't appeared bothered about her being there when she arrived and no one else was about either. The only thing that was different was a single rat that was scratching away at the dirt where the ducks and geese had been. This rat appeared no
different from any other rat she had seen, and so she didn't understand why the other animals had gone. She'd seen geese chase rats away plenty of times, but then again she thought that maybe it was just a coincidence and paid the thought no further attention. Lucy stood, brushed down her clothing with her hands, and then headed home.

***

Unlike Lucy, John had no choice but to attend school and this was his very first day. His parents had kept him at home for a week wanting him to adjust himself to the new town, and also so that others got used to seeing him. Those that were physically disabled in some way were always looked down on by others, and so he was particularly nervous about attending.

Thomas had wheeled him down in his barrow that morning and had left him with the schoolmistress who introduced herself as Mrs Grisham. The mistress awkwardly picked up the handles of the barrow and wheeled him to the front of the class where all the children of various ages gawped at him. As he sat in his barrow in front of the class, Mrs Grisham introduced him with her hard voice to the other children.

'This is master John Smith. As you can see he is a cripple, but please don't treat him any less than a normal person.'

A girl around ten years old put her hand up.

'What is it Patricia?' asked Mrs Grisham.

'What is a cripple?' she asked.

'Someone who can't walk dummy!' shouted a boy from across the classroom.

Mrs Grisham gave the boy a stern look.

'That's right Albert, but next time raise your hand!'

'Sorry Mrs,' replied the boy.

'Yes, he can't walk so please be careful that you don't trip over him!' said Mrs Grisham.

The children began to laugh.

'Cuthbert, wheel him to the cushions in the corner where he can sit,' instructed Mrs Grisham.

A short boy with brown hair and several cold sores on his lip got up and wheeled John over to a corner of the room where thick cushions and blankets were piled up. The boy helped John out of the barrow and onto the soft furnishings.

'Thank you,' said John.

The boy didn't acknowledge him, but just went back to his peers.

John made himself comfortable and glanced around the room to take in his surroundings. There were about thirty children of various ages and sizes and even three children with black skin. The room itself had various shelves that were half filled with books and there were also various wooden toys scattered around the room. Mrs Grisham sat in a rocking chair behind a small table in front of a blackboard. The blackboard was blank, although the chalk marks of previous words and drawings could vaguely be seen. Many children passed him without even glancing his way, however one boy literally tripped over and landed on top of him.

'I'm so sorry!' said the boy.

John noticed that the boy had a rag wrapped around his head covering his eyes.

'No problem,' replied John. 'Why are you wearing a rag over your eyes? Are you playing a game?

'No,' replied the boy. 'I'm blind!'

'I've never met a blind person before,' said John.

'Well, this is what we look like. Well, I think it is! I can't actually see to be sure,' he laughed.

John laughed with him.

'I'm John.'

'I'm William, but you can call me Will,' replied the boy.

'Nice to meet you, Will.'

'You too John! So you're the boy with no legs?'

'I do have legs! They just don't work.'

'Whys that?'

'I was just born that way. Legs broke when Ma gave birth to me and though they healed, they never worked.'

'What a bore!' said Will.

'What's the story with your eyes? Born like it?' asked John.

'No,' said Will shaking his head. 'Accident!'

'What happened?

'To be honest, I can't remember. I was helping the reverend at the church a few years ago and apparently, I slipped and fell head first onto a low metal spiked fence. I gouged my eyes out but fortunately, I survived. It's all hazy. Everything is a blank!'

'That's terrible!' said John. 'Don't you remember it?'

'No, don't remember a thing!'

'I'm so sorry Will.'

'It's not your fault!' laughed Will. 'Guess what though?'

'What?'

'We're all freaks round here Johnny!' said Will still laughing.

John laughed.

'Not really, but there is another one like us.'

'Who?' asked John.

'Alice. She's one of the slave girls.'

'Slave girls?'

'Yes, you know, the ones with black skin!'

'Of course!'

John looked around the room and saw the black girl Will was talking about. She was sitting alone and had a large piece of slate in her hand, and a piece of chalk in the other.

'What's wrong with her?' asked John.

'She's mute! Can't speak a word.'

'Really! That's so sad.'

'She writes on a piece of stone when she wants to say something, apparently.'

'You both friends?'

'Not really because we can't communicate properly. She can hear me but I can't read her words,' replied Will.

'We need to befriend her. She's all alone.'

'Okay John, let's do it.'

'If you put me in my barrow and push me, I'll direct you to her.'

'No problem!'

At that, Will bent and picked up John and put him in his barrow. John then directed him over to the girl named Alice. John noticed that the classroom was now very quiet. Most of the children had gone outside to play on the small area of grass that was called a playground. John could see some of the children running about, and a few more were laughing and playing together. Mrs Grisham had also gone outside and so very few remained in the room. The other two black-skinned children were close by and looked quizzically at Will pushing John toward Alice. As John approached he waved at the girl.

'Hello,' he said.

The girl waved back and then reached for her chalk and began to write on the piece of slate on her lap. She then held it up where John could see what she had written. It said, "Hello, I'm Alice."

The girl's handwriting was beautiful. It was neater and more graceful than any handwriting that John had seen before.

'I'm John, and this is Will.'

'Hi,' said Will. 'It's good to meet you.'

John and Alice laughed! Will wasn't even facing Alice, he was facing a nearby bookshelf.

'Who are you talking to Will?' laughed John. 'Alice is over here!'

Will turned to face her a little bashful.

'Sorry, Alice!'

Alice smiled at him.

'What are you doing!' shouted Mrs Grisham from the yard doorway. 'Get away from her!'

John turned toward her in shock as she came stomping over to the three of them.

'You are not to speak to her or any of her kind in my classroom,' she screamed.

'I'm sorry Mrs,' said Will apologetically. 'We were just being friendly!'

'Shut up William!'

'But.....'

Mrs Grisham then struck Will across the face causing him to fall back.

'Get out of here right now!'

Will got up and felt his way out of the classroom and into the yard. John could clearly see the blood dripping from his split lip. Mrs Grisham then grabbed the handles of John's barrow and wheeled him angrily away.

'As for you young John, you are to never do that again! If you do then I'll be forced to punish you just as I did to young William! Do you understand?'

'Yes Mrs Grisham,' John replied shaking.

Mrs Grisham then proceeded to stride over to Alice. She grabbed her by the arm and led her to a cupboard in the corner of the classroom. She then opened the door and pushed Alice inside. John could see the tears on Alice's face and the fear in her eyes as the cupboard door was closed on her and locked.

CHAPTER 4

THOMAS & OWEN

Thomas strode through the street like a man with a purpose, and he did have a purpose, he was going to tell Mrs Grisham exactly what he thought of her.

Thomas rarely became angry, but when it came to someone hurting or threatening either of his two younger siblings, he became more than just angry, he became furious. John had returned home from school and had told of the events that had happened and immediately Thomas acted. Despite the protests of his mother and father, Thomas walked straight out the door and strode furiously toward the small school. Even the cries of John and Lucy didn't dissuade him from going.

'How dare she!' he muttered to himself.

He played it over in his mind again, and again.

The woman had struck a blind child, splitting his lip, and then threatened to do the same to John if he misbehaved. The woman then went and locked a mute black child in a cupboard for three hours. For what? Being mute or being black! John said that the girl had been crying, and had stunk of urine when she had eventually been let out.

She's supposed to be looking after the children, especially those who are different or have physical issues! he thought. *She should be helping and encouraging them, not treating them like they're less than nothing!*

Thomas thought back to his auntie Emmy and the way she had spoken about John.

She may be a little loose with her tongue and have a habit of not thinking before she speaks, but at least there's no malice behind it!

Thomas neared the small building that the townsfolk called a school. Thomas could see the mistress pottering about through a window. She appeared to be picking up books and toys and tidying up. Thomas strode up to the door and entered through it without knocking. The mistress turned around startled.

'Who do you think you are!' shouted Thomas.

Mrs Grisham was taken aback by his loud, aggressive voice.

'Who do you think you are?' replied Mrs Grisham. 'You have no right to barge in here Master Smith! Kindly leave before I call the guards!'

'Not until you apologise to my brother, and the others that you hurt and scared! They're just children! It's not their fault they're different! They don't need some stuck-up old troll trying to make them feel less than what they are!'

'How dare you! Leave at once!'

'No! It's petty-minded fools like you that make this world a terrible place! You claim to follow Christ, but where are your love and compassion!'

'You don't know anything about me and you will keep my love of Christ out of this!'

'You're a hypocrite!' Thomas yelled.

Mrs Grisham slapped Thomas clean across the face. The strike was not enough to hurt him, but enough to stifle his anger. It was then that the strangest thing happened. Mrs Grisham broke down in tears. She literally curled up on the floor and began to rock herself, and sob hysterically. Thomas walked into the school expecting many things, but this was not one of them. He expected her to shout, even to hit him, and maybe even to storm out, but he never expected her to break down and cry. Thomas was visibly shocked and didn't know what to say or do. So Thomas did the only thing he knew he could do. He left.

Thomas strode out of the school and headed back home. As Thomas walked he felt a mixture of emotions. On the one hand, he had taught her a lesson and told her some home truths. On the other hand, though, he never expected her to start crying. Maybe there was more to this woman, and why she treated the children this way. Thomas had a feeling that he'll have plenty of time to think about it. After all, he was now in trouble.

Ten minutes after Thomas arrived home the guards came knocking. Thomas was hauled up to the town lockup where he spent the night shivering in the cold without food, water, or a blanket. As Thomas was curled up in the corner of the lockup he went over it again, and again, and came to the same conclusion every time.

No one threatens my family!

***

Owen sat in the tavern nursing a pint of mead. He knew he shouldn't be there but he desperately needed a drink. Thomas had been dragged up to the town lockup for his terrible behaviour that day. Owen had then followed behind and tried to plead Thomas' case, but both he and Thomas received a good telling off from Captain Long, head of the Brading Town guard. Captain Long was a short man and Owen had liked him at first. Not now though!

Long in name, short in legs! Owen had thought to himself.

Following his telling off, Owen had then headed home, but as soon he saw the Kyngs Arms he licked his lips and quickly entered the tavern. It was only about four o'clock, but there were a fair number of patrons that had already started drinking.

'Mr Smith!,' cried Mr Cooper the tavern keeper. 'I was wondering when you were finally going to grace us with your presence!'

'Go easy on me Charlie!' replied Owen. 'It been a tough few days. I just need a bit of a pick-me-up. I ain't fallen off the wagon yet. Just need to wet m' whistle. If you knows what I mean.'

'No problem. I'll get Mavis to bring you a pint over.'

'Thanks, Charlie.'

At that, Owen went and sat at a quiet table away from the windows. He dare not be seen after his vow to stay off the drink but he'd worked really hard over the past few days and hadn't drunk a drop for two weeks. He knew he had made a promise, but he reasoned that Mary probably wouldn't mind. True, she'd nag and moan but then she would forgive him as she always did. Besides, it was just a one-off he reminded himself, it's not like she'd find out.

One pint, then I'll go, he thought to himself.

One of the serving girls, whom Owen presumed to be Mavis, came with a pint of mead and placed it in front of him on the table.

'Thanks, sweetheart!' said Owen.

She smiled at him and gave him a wink, then headed back toward the bar.

She be sweet that one! thought Owen looking at the serving girl as she walked away.

Owen took a long gulp of the cool brown ale. He could feel the liquid trickling down the inside of his throat and into his belly. It warmed his bones. He finished the pint quickly and felt a little happier for it. He'd missed the feeling of a good drink inside him, and how it relieved all the stresses of life. After a couple of pints of the good stuff, it felt like you were floating and everything was peaceful. It was pure bliss, and nothing could beat that feeling.

Owen called out to the barmen, 'Bring me another pint Charlie!'

The barmen gave a thumbs up.

Matthew Ryan

I better not drink too much! thought Owen. *I wouldn't want the other half to catch on, she'd go nuts! Also, we have church tomorrow so I better not stay out too late!*

CHAPTER 5

LUCY & JOHN

"Children are best seen and not heard, and girls even more so!" That's what Ma used to always say to Lucy, but Lucy had a problem with this. Despite being only thirteen years old she always had a lot to say. She looked at the world around her and had questions like, why is the sky blue? Why does the sun always rise in the East and set in the West? And why do rivers always flow into the sea? She also had many other questions like, why are men viewed as superior to women? Why are those in power always bad? And why would anyone ever want to get married?

Lucy was a thinker, but worse than that, she said what she thought. Pa blamed this on her mother. Ma had taught her to read and write from an early age, and always encouraged her to think outside the box. And this was exactly what Lucy did, much to her father's disgust. It did even annoy her mother at times too.

The family had arrived home after another church service. Ma and Pa were busy cleaning out the stable, trying to make it more comfortable for the donkey. They were also making minor repairs on things around the home and had roped Thomas in too. Lucy thought it would be better for her to leave before she was given a task to do too. Her Pa shouted after her but she pretended not to hear and quickly scarpered. She slipped out of the house, ducked around a corner, and then purposefully lost herself among the other cottages and huts. She headed East toward the river Yar.

Lucy arrived a few minutes later, and to her, it looked just as perfect as every other time she had been there. The day was beautiful. The sun was bright with not a cloud in the sky, but there was also a cool breeze that was refreshing to breathe in.

Lucy loved the river and had visited it several times since first arriving. She especially liked the small island in the middle of the river. It was overgrown with scrubs and bushes, but in the middle was a patch of grass not three yards square with a young birch tree growing in the middle. Time and again Lucy would wade through the river to the island where she would watch the events that happened on the bridges and in the areas along the riverbank. She had seen many funny sights of drunken men and nagging women, and even a cock fight or two.

Today, she lifted her dress and waded into the river trying not to let her dress get wet. She reached the island and settled down on the patch of grass and began to think about life and especially about the priest's sermon that she heard earlier that day. This time it was about the interloper. It troubled her to think that someone was near at hand watching and waiting to strike at a sinner. Were they watching her now? The thought gave her goose pimples. She laid back on the grass feeling the sun on her face and relaxed. Within a few minutes, Lucy drifted off to sleep.

Lucy was awoken by a terrible high-pitched screech. She sat up quickly getting her bearings. It was still bright, she must have only drifted off to sleep for a short time. She could not see the source of the strange sound until it happened again. It was a ginger cat! It was hunkered up in an aggressive stance.

Wow, she thought. *A catfight.*

They were always exciting. When two cats fought, it was a flurry of claws and fur, and it was a real sight to behold. Lucy looked to see the other cat, but there wasn't one. All she could see was a rat. It was a very large rat, but still only a rat. Why did the cat simply not just pounce? It could easily dispatch of the rat with no problem, but then she saw something else. She saw another rat and another. There were three large rats moving slowly toward the cat ready to strike. The cat was hunkered up, not because it was about to attack, but because it had nowhere to run. It was backed up against the river and was surrounded.

Lucy was suddenly terrified and feared for the cat. She got to her feet and saw a nearby stone that was large enough to scare the rats away. She aimed and threw the rock at the rats. Her aim was true, but the outcome was not what she expected. Instead of scaring the rats away, it scared the cat. The cat jumped in shock and ran for it. The rats, however, were on the cat in two heartbeats. One jumped at the cat's throat and was tearing it out. Another was ripping away at the cat's stomach, and the third scratched away at its back and bit on the cat's ears. The sight was absolutely terrifying. Lucy opened her mouth to scream, but nothing came out. She watched in horror as the rats quickly killed the cat and then began to pull its dead, limp body along the ground. The three rats worked as one and dragged the cat to a nearby hole along the riverbank, and then dragged the cat underground. Lucy looked on in shock and horror and saw the bloody trail leading to the hole.

Lucy immediately broke down in tears and curled up on the floor in fear. She began to shake uncontrollably. Everything was silent except for the river. Not a sound could be heard, not even the sound of a bird. She felt eyes on her from everywhere and felt trapped.

Lucy laid there for what felt like hours. To her horror, she heard the sound of water splashing. Something was coming toward her through the river. She jumped up afraid that the rats had come for her, but to her surprise and relief, it was Thomas.

'I thought you were here, little Sis,' Thomas said.

Lucy immediately ran to her brother and burst into tears.

'What's wrong?' he asked. 'Did someone hurt you?'

'Oh Thomas! It was terrible, so terrible!' she sobbed.

Thomas picked her up and carried her back across the river.

'Let's get you home, and you can tell us what happened,' he said soothingly.

***

John felt sorry for Lucy. It had been over a week since the sighting of the rat attack, but despite her protests and obvious distress, no one believed her. Ma and Pa wanted to believe her, but the Mayor and the priest both said that she must have been half asleep when it happened. They reassured Lucy that rats do not act the way that she described. They said it must have been another cat or maybe she just dreamt it. Either way, Lucy wasn't happy. In fact, she was more than unhappy, she was angry and also a little scared. Over the past week, she had barely left the house but when she did she was anxious. Every time she saw a rat she panicked.

This was not the Lucy he had grown to love and admire. This headstrong girl was now a quivering wreck. Thomas tried to comfort her and reassure her. He seemed to be the only one who really believed what she said. Like a parent, Thomas comforted her during her distress.

'You shouldn't treat her like a baby,' Pa would say. 'She needs to grow up lad.'

Ma was little better simply saying things like 'She'll get over it,' and, 'She brought it on herself,' but Thomas looked after her, and John tried to help too.

It was another day of school for John. John enjoyed it because he was now overlooked by the mistress. After Thomas had shouted at her, she had left him, Will, and Alice to their own devices. John enjoyed the company of his two companions.

John got to learn a little more about the girl named Alice. She was black-skinned and was about ten years old, but she was completely mute. She was one of the children of the slaves that worked at Barton Manor. Mr and Mrs Barton treated their slaves well and wanted the children to have an education, and so they were allowed to attend school. Alice was seldom allowed to associate with others, except at school, but now and then she was allowed out under the watchful care of one of her older siblings.

The three children became fast friends, and so John really enjoyed his time at school.

On this particular day, the three children were in the small yard of the school. They had placed a ceramic pot about three yards away from them and each would take turns throwing stones to make them land inside. Will hated this game, obviously because he couldn't see, but his lack of sight caused his stones to end up in the funniest of places. The last time they played this game he had managed to smash a plant pot, hit a rat, and also land a stone in the school mistresses apron.

Today, Alice was winning, scoring three stones to John's one, and William's none. It was William's turn again and he threw a small stone that hit a cat sitting on a nearby wall. The cat shrieked and dashed off leaving John and Alice laughing, and Will confused.

'What happened?' asked Will.

'Didn't you hear?' replied John. 'You hit a cat and it ran off hissing and screaming!'

'Oh!' laughed Will. 'I thought a rat had scared it off!'

'A rat? What do you mean?'

'I heard that it's happened a few times now. The cats keep running away from the rats. The cats in this town must be getting lazy!'

'How strange,' John replied.

Alice then tugged on John's arm. She then began to draw on her slate a picture of a cat being chased by a rat. She pointed at the cat and then pointed at herself.

'What's she saying?' asked Will.

'I think she's trying to tell us that she had a cat that was chased by a rat.'

Alice then rubbed the cat out with her sleeve and drew a question mark.

'I think she's also trying to tell us that her cat is now missing.'

'Maybe we should help her go look for it.' said Will.

'Great idea, but what help can you be? You can't even see!' joked John.

'I'll push you in your barrow and you can look with Alice.'

'I like it,' said John enthusiastically.

John helped Alice to understand the plan and the three sneakily set off when the mistress wasn't looking. Will carried John to his barrow, under the guidance of John, and put him inside. The three then set off together on their own little adventure.

Alice walked ahead with the two boys following closely behind. She led them to a grassy knoll not a hundred yards from her own home and pointed to a stone wall with brambles and thickets on the opposite side. Using her hands she indicated that the cat had run along being chased by a rat and that the cat had then jumped over the wall and landed among the thickets, but she had also indicated that the rat had done the same thing in pursuit. John explained to Will what Alice had seen and directed Will to the wall.

As the two boys reached the wall they both heard a strange noise coming from the thicket behind the wall. John sat up more fully in the barrow and reached for the short stone wall. With all the strength he had in his arms, John heaved himself up so that he could peer over the wall.

Again the noise was heard and the thicket rustled with movement. John was curious, though a little frightened, but wanted to keep his cool in front of Will and Alice. He tried to see through the thicket in between the thorns and thistles. He saw something black moving about. Maybe this was Alice's cat! It probably jumped over the wall and hurt itself when landing.

'I see something!' cried John.

'What is it?' asked Will.

'I'm not sure! I need a better look!'

John reached into the thicket pushing leaves and branches aside as he went. He was close to touching the black creature when suddenly, it jumped up at him. John was thrown back and landed on the floor, more shocked than hurt. He looked up to see a blackbird squawking angrily as it flew away from them heading west.

'It was just a bird!' laughed John. 'The little blighter scared me half to death!'

Will and Alice both laughed hysterically. John laughed along with them as Will helped him back into the barrow.

'There's nothing there!' said John still laughing. 'Your cat probably ran off further into the thicket.'

They decided to head back before they got into trouble and agreed to look for the cat again in the next few days.

In the thicket, not two yards from where John had looked were two big rats eating the remains of a cat.

CHAPTER 6

THOMAS & OWEN

The second rat attack sighting came three days after the first. Thomas had been asked by uncle Rupert to deliver a box of horseshoes to farmer Giles on the East side of the river Yar. The box of horseshoes was placed on a small cart that was attached to an old horse who had seen too many winters. Thomas mounted the cart and guided the horse out of the smithy stable, and up the Mall Road heading South out of town. As Thomas was moving along he saw various townsfolk whom he had met over the past few weeks. All gave him customary nods and good mornings. The town appeared to have accepted them despite the family only living there for a short time.

As Thomas continued up Mall Road he saw something that would change him forever more. It was a girl. She looked about his age and he thought her the most beautiful thing he had ever seen. The girl was feeding chickens from an apron that she had pulled up to her waist. She plunged her hand into the apron, took seeds, and then scattered them on the ground. The chickens were pecking eagerly and clucking encouragement to the girl.

Thomas stopped the horse and simply sat staring at the girl. He was mesmerised by the way her long blonde hair moved around in the breeze and how it at times clung to her tight bodice. Thomas felt a stirring in his loins that he had never felt before. Many of the girls he had grown up around had never made him feel like that, but this girl was different. She was special. Unfortunately for Thomas, the girl had seen him staring at her and so gave him a wave. Thomas blushed and nervously waved back. He was very embarrassed and thought he had better move on quickly.

'Aren't you going to say hello?' the girl shouted.

Thomas was torn. He had two options. Option one was to simply ride on pretending he hadn't heard her. Option two was to get off the cart and head over to her. Unfortunately, he subconsciously went with a different option, which was to simply sit there dumbfounded. Before he realised what was happening, she had walked toward him and was nearly at his cart.

'I don't think you heard me,' she said. 'Aren't you going to say hello?'

'I'm so sorry, I didn't hear you. I was....er....distracted!'

'Distracted? By what?'

He needed a good reason for sitting there looking stupid.

'I was counting your chickens!'

Counting your chickens! he thought to himself. *How stupid did that sound!*

'Really? How many did you count? She asked.

'Twenty-seven!'

'Twenty-seven? We only have eight!'

'Bizarre isn't it!' he laughed.

The girl laughed too.

'I've seen you about,' she said. 'You intrigued me.'

'What do you mean?'

'I wanted to know who you were, so I followed you a few times.'

'So it was you that was spying on me?'

'Guilty as charged,' she laughed.

'My name is Thomas, my family and I moved here a few weeks ago. What's your name?'

'That's for me to know, and for you to find out.' She winked.

At that, she began to walk off back toward her chickens.

'See you around, Thomas.' She laughed, glancing back at him.

'I hope so!' he replied longingly.

She then blew him a kiss and ran back up the field. Thomas quickly got the horse and cart moving and headed toward his delivery address.

He turned eastward and the road began to lead downward toward a crossroads. He carried on Eastward and began to head toward the bridge over the river Yar. He sat in the seat thinking about the beautiful girl he had just seen.

'I think I'm in love!' he said out loud to nobody in particular.

He thought about a way he could see her again. Maybe he could ride back the way he came and hope she was still in the field, but then again, he didn't want to appear strange and desperate. Then again he thought wouldn't it be strange if he didn't return the way he came? His mind was moving a thousand miles per hour thinking about the what-ifs. He was so distracted that he almost missed the events of what happened at the watchtower by the bridge.

On the town side of the bridge, a watchtower had been erected many years ago. The French had previously tried to invade England, and the Wyght island proved to be a good landing spot for French infantry. And so watchtowers with large bells had been erected throughout the island with watchmen assigned to keep a constant lookout. The watchman assigned today was a man in his fifties. He had thick red hair and a long red beard and spoke with a strong Northern accent. His name was Montgomery but was simply known to the locals as Monty.

As Thomas approached the bridge and the watchtower, he saw Monty fall headfirst to the ground. The sound of broken bones cracking stirred Thomas from his daydreaming, and the sound of screaming from nearby women brought Thomas completely back to reality. Thomas jumped out of the cart and ran toward Monty. The man was bloody and broken, He was alive, but only barely.

'The rats! The rats!' he screamed before he passed out.

Thomas saw the broken form of the man who had fallen fifty feet from the tower. His arms and legs were broken in several places and he was bleeding from both of his nostrils and one of his ears. What Thomas noticed that disturbed him, even more, were the great chunks of flesh that had been ripped out at various points from Monty's legs. It looked as though Monty had sustained a frenzied attack by a creature, or several creatures, and this probably led to his falling or jumping from the tower.

Thomas quickly took Monty in his arms and tried to rouse him. He shouted to the women who were crying and screaming a few yards away.

'Get help!'

One of the women ran off, and a few minutes later a group of guards arrived. The guards lifted Monty onto Thomas' cart and led it back into town. Thomas followed behind, a little shaken, and a little perplexed.

Why did Monty fall from the tower and what could have caused those injuries to the man's body? Thomas thought. *Monty had cried out that it was rats! Those bites were bigger than anything a rat could do, but then again, what about what Lucy had seen? She said the rats that she saw kill that cat were bigger than normal. Could these be the very same rats that Lucy had seen that day by the river? It was only a hundred yards away from where he was now. Maybe the two cases were linked.*

When Monty was taken from the cart in town he was already dead. Thomas was questioned, and so were the women that had also seen the incident. Thomas headed home later that day with the horseshoes still in the back of the cart and the thought of the mysterious girl temporarily lost.

***

The day of the funeral was dreary. The clouds were heavy in the sky, but the rain was holding back. There was a deep, dark sense of loss among the folks of Brading. Monty was a very happy and charismatic chap who was generous toward those that had very little. He was well-loved and many of the townsfolk attended his funeral.

Owen and Mary attended the service along with Thomas. The other two children were left at home with instructions not to get into any trouble. As the three stood in the graveyard in the cold morning air listening to Reverend Nicholas, and his interpretation of what heaven and hell really were, Owen felt tired. He wished he was in the Kyngs Arms sipping a mug of something special beside the tavern fire.

Who likes funerals? he thought to himself. *The person's dead and we all have to keep on living. No time to mourn, there were things to do such as earning money and preparing for the town festival which was fast approaching.*

Owen was disturbed from his thoughts by the reverend who claimed strongly that they were actually living in hell on earth now. Owen didn't like this so-called priest. He was horrible, to say the least. In fact, Owen would have gone so far as to say he was grotesque. He was morally, physically, and spiritually a disgusting piece of filth, but Owen knew that he needed to love his neighbour which unfortunately included the reverend Nicolas.

Owen looked around the graveyard. He saw many of the principal men of the town and their wives. There were also many of the Brading Town guards in attendance and also other key families. All looked completely devastated by the death of Monty. Owen had only met Monty once but felt it right that he, Mary, and Thomas attend the burial. Thomas after all had been a witness to the terrible event and had helped bring Monty home.

Owen reflected on what had happened. He and uncle Rupert were working in the smithy. They were really busy! Uncle had said that business was booming since Owen had joined him. Yesterday afternoon, however, was busier than normal. He remembered Thomas walking into the smithy all sullen-faced carrying the box of horseshoes he was sent out with. He remembered scalding Thomas verbally for not making the delivery even after hearing what had happened. He told Thomas that he should have carried on and minded his own business.

Owen also didn't believe that rats were involved. He told Thomas that Monty must have been delirious after falling from such a great height. Besides, rats were not big creatures that could inflict the wounds Thomas had described. Owen had lived with rats around him his whole life, and never had he ever seen one that could do such a thing. Rats didn't go out there way to attack people either. True one might nip you if you got too close, but most paid no attention. Owen did feel though that the town of Brading did have a rat problem. In all the towns and villages he had ever lived in, here had the most rats. This still didn't prove anything, and so he was happy to dismiss Thomas. Even when Thomas reminded him of what had happened with Lucy, Owen was still not convinced.

Owen listened as the reverend ended the service, said a prayer, and then closed his Bible. The people there began to mingle with one another with Monty, and the nature of his death, understandably being the key talking point. Mary and Thomas were talking with farmer Giles' wife when Lord Mulberry suddenly came over to speak to Owen.

'Good morning my Lord,' said Owen respectfully.

'Good morning to you sir. Such a sad moment is a funeral wouldn't you agree?' asked the Mayor.

'Absolutely my Lord. Life is fleeting, even for the best of us.'

'It was good of your son to help poor Monty.'

'Thank you. We have always told our children to be like the good Samaritan. Help others whenever you are able to do so.'

'Good for you. I wish there were more honest folk like you in town.'

'Thank you, my Lord.'

'I was wondering if you would be able to do me a small favour Mr Smith if that is ok?'

'Of course my Lord. What do you need of me?'

'Well as you know, we have the town festival this coming Saturday and I need the sacrificial bull collected from Lady Barton's grounds at the rear of her manor. Would you be able to collect the bull on Friday evening, take it to the bull ring in town, and secure it ready for the festival?' asked the Mayor.

'Of course,' replied Owen. 'I'll take Thomas with me, he'd be happy to help.'

'Thank you, Mr Smith, I deeply appreciate it. I'll inform Lady Barton that you will collect it Friday evening.'

'Absolutely, whatever suits you and her my Lord.'

'Thank you again,' said the Mayor as he walked away.

Great! thought Owen. *Another job to do!*

CHAPTER 7

MARY & LUCY

It was the Friday before the festival and Mary were extremely busy. She had attended this festival a few times in the past with her family, but she had never been involved in preparing for it. She was currently putting up bunting in the main town square along with aunt Emmy. She loved aunt Emmy but many thought the old woman was very odd. She was constantly complaining about anything and everything, and she was a gossip too. She knew everything about everyone.

As the two were tying up some bunting over the town hall entrance, the Mayor walked past and gave them a brief greeting before quickly moving on.

'That be a strange one that,' said aunt Emmy. 'Lord Mulberry? More like Lord of the privy!'

'What do you mean auntie?' asked Mary.

'He's a nobody, that's what I means!'

'He is a Lord though, isn't he?'

'Yes, yes, but there are Lords and then there are ones like him.'

'You're speaking in riddles auntie, explain yourself.'

'Lord Mulberry be the adopted son of the Asprey lady. She be the one that lives in the big manor house outside town. He only be Mayor cos of her influence. He truly is useless. With all the problems in this here town, all he can do is strut around parading his stupid hats, waistcoats, and gold.'

'Is that why there are so many rats?' Mary asked. 'Because he won't deal with it.'

'Yep, don't want to spend the coin needed. Every year it be something new. Last year it was the sewage running through the town. Took nigh on three months before he got off his backside to do something. The sewage still isn't right now!'

'Do you think the bad sewage is what's causing the problem with the rats?'

'Probably,' replied Aunt Emmy.

'There is a serious problem here,' said Mary. 'I mean there have always been rats around, but in this town, they're everywhere, and these ones don't even bother to hide. They don't care who goes near them.'

'That be true my dear, but just do what I do. Give 'em a good whack with ya broom!'

'I'll keep that in mind auntie,' laughed Mary.

The two finished tying the bunting around the town hall and moved to start on the tavern. Mary remembered being told that the Kyngs Arms was one of the busiest taverns on this side of the Wyght island. Sailors would pull into the harbour down the way at the haven docks and would walk 500 yards up to the town, to sit out a storm at the tavern or simply to wait until unloading was done at the dock. Many men frequented this tavern and fortunately, Mary's husband was not one of them. He'd been clean of drink now for about a month and she was pleased.

Mary never understood what the fascination was with going to a tavern. Was it simply for the taste of ale, or was it just to get away from the family? Then again it was probably because of the serving girls. They truly disgusted Mary, the way they flirted with the men, flashing their ankles and even shoulders. They were wenches as far as she was concerned. No woman should ever do anything like that, and that truly was Mary's belief. Mary's beliefs no doubt came from her upbringing.

She was the daughter of a maid serving in one of the big houses on the West side of the island. She had learned her letters and was even able to write, a skill even her husband had refused to learn. She had been destined to serve in a house like her mother before her, but upon meeting Owen, and listening to his dreams of fame and fortune, she gave it all up to be with him. Her life quickly went downhill from there. Now she was a wife, and a mother to three children, who were scraping a living to make ends meet. Regardless though, she still had her beliefs and morals.

As they were tying the bunting outside the Kyngs Arms, aunt Emmy called out to Mary.

'Look who's in there while we be working hard?'

'Who?' asked Mary.

'Our Owen!' she replied. 'He's a right lazy so and so!'

Mary's heart dropped. She was completely shocked. She peered through the window hoping that aunt Emmy was wrong, but immediately recognised him. Without thinking, Mary stormed into the tavern.

It was early evening and so the tavern was starting to get very busy. There were dozens of men drinking and women serving, and many were singing along to a song being played on a piano. Mary noted that the piano was seriously out of tune as she pushed her way past the patrons. She found Owen propped up at the bar with a flagon of ale in one hand and a serving girl in the other. Mary grabbed him by his ear causing Owen to yelp and drop his drink. The contents of the flagon spilled onto the serving girl causing her to screech and fall from Owen's lap. Mary then began dragging Owen outside to the amusement and laughter of all those that saw what happened.

'What the heck are you doing Pa!' she ranted. 'You said you'd given up the drink! I can't believe I listened to your lies again. You're also supposed to be running an errand for Lord Mulberry ready for the festival tomorrow! Don't you remember?'

'I know pudding but I was thirty.....I mean thirsty,' he replied, as he swayed about.

'You are expected at Lady Barton's at any time! You need to go now! Go get Thomas to help you, and go collect the bull before you're late. We can talk about this later!'

'You better leave now Owen my lad,' said aunt Emmy. 'It's a long walk!'

'I'm going, I'm going,' replied Owen.

He began to walk off with a slight uneasiness but he remained fairly straight on the path.

'Men!' laughed aunt Emmy.

'They're useless, especially that one!' declared Mary.

'They do have their uses though!' cackled aunt Emmy hysterically.

Mary laughed with her and the two continued working until the sun had set, but Mary was truly disappointed with Owen.

After the two women had finished working several hours later, they both said their goodbyes and parted ways. Aunt Emmy and uncle Rupert lived in one of the houses near the town square, so aunt Emmy did not have very far to go in order to get home. Mary, on the other hand, had to walk about 200 yards through town to get back to the cottage. Mary decided to pass by the bull ring to make sure Owen had done his job.

Mary walked up the main street and counted the rats. She counted about 30 rats before giving up and focussing on her destination. She passed several men and women who all gave customary greetings. As Mary approached the bull ring she could clearly see the bull chained up. It paid her no attention and simply ate at a nearby pile of hay.

He's done his job, thought Mary. *At least that's something!*

Suddenly, Mary heard snoring. She looked behind the pile of hay that the bull was eating from and saw Owen asleep on the floor with an empty flagon in his hand. He looked completely out of it. Mary moved over to him to try to wake him, but he was dead to the world. He snored happily and did not even stir.

He's going to regret drinking too much and sleeping there, thought Mary. *He's going to wake up with a terrible hangover and a bad back, and it will be nobody's fault but his!*

Mary left Owen to sleep in the hay next to the bull and hoped he would apologise for his actions and make it up to her the next day. Mary began to walk home ready to feed the children and relax. She wanted everybody to be ready for the exciting festivities that were to be held the next day, and she didn't want anything to ruin it.

***

Lucy was awoken on the day of the festival by the sound of banging on the front door. She had gone to sleep very late the night before due to the excitement of the festival. She remembered lying in her bed with the thoughts of the next day going round and round her head. She was looking forward to the games, the music, and the dancing. She was also excited about the food and drink. She hoped that she could even get a drink of a tipple of some kind from one of the serving girls from the tavern if she played her cards right. It had taken her what felt like many hours to finally fall asleep, but when she did, the dream was far from pleasurable.

Lucy dreamt about the festival, picturing the various stalls with their various games and food. She had dreamt of the children dancing in the town square as a fiddler played a fast-paced jig on his fiddle. She dreamt of the men drinking and the women eating. Then the dream went strange.

A dark cloud began to build up above the town and thunder could be heard. Suddenly, it began to rain literal cats and dogs. Lucy remembered everyone laughing and clapping as the dogs and cats landed on the floor. As the animals landed, however, they were dead. The vision and sound of bones breaking and blood spilling was all around, and the crowd still laughed and clapped. Lucy remembered the bodies of the animals piling up around her, so covered her eyes from the terrible sight. When she opened them again the dogs and cats were gone but something was different. The people around her looked different. They all had the heads of rats, and every single one of them stopped what they were doing and turned to look at her. Each began to grin a sharp-toothed smile at her. The rat people then ran toward her as she screamed.

Lucy had been awoken at that moment by the banging on the front door. The banging came again more furious and a man's voice was heard.

'Open up immediately!'

Thomas had jumped up out of bed to open the door. Standing on the other side of the door were three men of the Brading town guard and the Mayor. The Mayor barged his way past Thomas into the cottage.

'Where is your father?' he said impatiently.

Thomas shrugged

'I don't know!

'Then where is your mother?'

'We haven't seen either of them since yesterday.'

The Mayor motioned to one of the guards.

'Check the house!'

'What's this about?' asked Thomas.

'Your father is a thief!' replied the Mayor. 'He has stolen the bull that was going to be used at the festival! No doubt to feed you wretched lot!

'They're not here my Lord' said the guard who had looked around the cottage.

'When you see your father lad, you tell him that I'll make sure he hangs for what he's done!' said the Mayor in an extremely angry voice.

At that, the Mayor and guards stormed out leaving the front door wide open.

Thomas quickly looked around outside, and then shut the door.

'Where are Ma and Pa?' asked John.

'I don't know,' replied Thomas. 'Have you seen them, Lucy?'

'No,'

'Lucy, you and I will go out to look for them. John, you stay, and if they come home tell them what happened.'

'No problem,' said John.

'Where should we look?' asked Lucy.

'I'll head to aunt Emmy and check the smithy. You go look in town, especially the tavern,'

'Good idea,' Lucy replied.

The two got ready and went out to look for their parents.

Lucy headed toward the town square and the Kyngs Arms tavern. It was only around seven o'clock in the morning, but the streets were already getting busy. As Lucy continued on her way, she passed by the bull ring where she saw a terrible sight. The whole area was covered in blood. There were a few town guards who were stationed by the bull ring, and there were several women that Lucy recognised trying to clean up the mess. Lucy felt vomit rushing up from her stomach and began to retch. The smell was disgusting, and the sight was terrible to behold. Not only was their blood all over the pen but also bits of flesh and bone that Lucy presumed were parts of the bull. The rope that was used to tie the beast sat loosely in a puddle of blood.

One of the guards recognised Lucy.

'Hey, you! Look at what your father did!'

Lucy opened her mouth to speak but then closed it again. Nothing she could say would be of any use. Lucy saw behind the women who were cleaning that several rats were eating part of what appeared to be the bull's hind leg. Lucy began to gag again and so quickly ran off.

Lucy was confused. She presumed that when they said that her father had stolen the bull, the bull ring would simply be empty. She didn't understand why there was blood everywhere. And why were there bits of the beast's flesh and bone scattered about? It didn't make any sense. The only logical thing she could think of was that maybe her father had killed the beast and taken it somewhere, but why would he do that? And how could he move such a large dead animal? Lucy was truly baffled. What worried her most though, was where her mother and father were right now.

Where could they be? she thought.

Lucy approached the Kyngs Arms and stepped through the door. It was very empty in the tavern apart from the bartender who was cleaning the bar, and a serving girl cleaning a table.

Lucy approached the bar.

'Hey missy, you shouldn't be in here!' said the bartender.

'I'm sorry Mr Cooper, sir. I'm trying to find my father. Have you seen him?'

'No miss,' he then turned to the serving girl. 'Have you seen this girl's pa Dixie?'

'He was in ere last night but got dragged out by your ma, love!' Dixie replied.

'Thank you,' said Lucy.

At that, she turned and left the tavern while Mr Cooper and Dixie carried on with their chores.

Lucy stood outside the tavern trying to think of where her parents could be. She was about to head to her aunt Emmy's when suddenly several rats scurried past her feet. Lucy froze! One of the rats stopped and sniffed at her shoes. It then began to sniff her ankles. Lucy could feel the rat's whiskers tickling her legs as the rat sniffed further up her legs. Lucy could feel the sharp claws of the rat's paws as it lent on her shin and sniffed further up. Lucy began to shake and could feel her heart hammering rapidly in her chest. Tears began to run down her face. She couldn't move. She was petrified!

From nowhere, a broom came down hard on the rat causing it to run off. The person holding the broom was aunt Emmy. Lucy ran and grabbed hold of her.

'Don't worry dearest,' soothed aunt Emmy. 'It's gone now.'

Lucy let go and wiped the tears away from her face with the backs of her hands.

'What are you doing out so early?'

'I'm looking for Ma and Pa, auntie. Have you seen them?'

'No my lovely, not since yesterday. Last I saw was that your pa went to collect the bull for the festival, and your ma went home. Did no one come home last night?'

'No, the Mayor and the guards are looking for Pa! They came asking for him this morning, and Ma hasn't been home since yesterday.'

'Very strange. I wonder what they want with your Pa.'

'It has something to do with the bull he collected.'

'Interesting,' said aunt Emmy. 'Come with me child, and tell me everything.'

At that, the two began to walk back to Lucy's home. On the way, Lucy told aunt Emmy everything she knew.

CHAPTER 8

JOHN & OWEN

John was growing restless. Thomas and Lucy had only been gone about an hour, but he was already feeling agitated. He'd just chased out another rat, the third since they left, which is no easy task when you can't walk.

John sat thinking about his parents. He was seriously worried about them. They were never the most loving of folks a child could have, but he did love them and appreciate all that they did for them. When it came to parenting, he and Lucy were more drawn to Thomas. Thomas was a great substitute parent. He always made time for them and they both loved him very much.

His father was a good man at heart but he had a serious drinking problem. John had heard from both Thomas and Lucy that Pa had been secretly visiting the Kyngs Arms. His visits were apparently becoming more frequent and sooner, or later, their mother would find out. Pa had said that moving here would be a new start, but the new start hadn't lasted very long. He had fallen back into doing what he loved most.

John reflected on his mother. She was a good woman and completely devoted to God, but she was not an affectionate mother. She was always preoccupied with other things. She was always worrying about the future and the worst that could happen. She also constantly worried about money, and so worked even harder than their father.

John's thoughts about his parents were interrupted by the door opening. Thomas, Lucy, and aunt Emmy walked in.

'No sign of them?' asked John.

'No,' replied aunt Emmy with a look of worry on her face. 'Your Pa is probably sleeping off a hangover somewhere, but I don't know what could've happened to ya Ma. It is a worry lad.'

'Lucy and I checked everywhere we knew, but no joy,' said Thomas.

'What should we do now aunt Emmy?' asked Lucy.

'Nowt much we can do sweetie but keep waiting,' she replied.

Thomas and Lucy sat down with their heads in their hands. John began to well up. He loved his Ma and Pa. He began to get upset and so Thomas went and hugged him. Aunt Emmy simply potted around the house tidying up and cleaning where needed.

It had been about two hours when the news finally came. Lucy had slept during that time, while Thomas sat in one of the high-back chairs near the now dead fireplace. He appeared lost in his own thoughts. John had simply sat looking out the window. He had seen dozens of rats milling about in the street. He saw one rat who climbed along the roof of a nearby cottage. The rat was going to pounce on a pigeon that had landed there some minutes earlier, but the rat failed. The bird saw the rat approaching and simply flew off.

Aunt Emmy was sitting on the doorstep darning some socks when the news came in the form of uncle Rupert. John had always thought uncle Rupert a funny-looking man. He was short with large boils and blisters on his face. He also had a bright red nose from being a heavy drinker. He was another one that was known for frequenting the Kyngs Arms more often than he should. After briefly talking with aunt Emmy, uncle Rupert stepped into the house to relay the news.

'Hello, children. I'm afraid that your mother and father have still not been found!'

Lucy burst into tears. Thomas moved toward her to hug and comfort her. John sat there confused.

'The town guards were sent out to conduct a thorough search of the town and the surrounding area, but found nothing,' Rupert said.

'What's going to happen now?' asked John.

'The Mayor is going to arrange for more searches to be done,' replied uncle Rupert. 'There is still a chance your Ma and Pa will be found.'

'So what happens to us? What do we do now?' asked Thomas.

'You're coming home with us,' replied aunt Emmy. 'We have plenty of room back at the house, but ya got to pull your weight, all of ya! I'm sure your Ma and Pa be back soon but I ain't waiting on ya. Auntie and Uncle too old to be caring for nippers!'

'We won't be any trouble,' said Thomas. 'We really appreciate your kindness.'

Both Lucy and John also gave their thanks.

'Let's get your things together children,' said uncle Rupert. 'You won't need much. It'll no doubt only be for a short time.'

John hoped that uncle Rupert was right about his mother and father. As he looked around the room he saw the many things that reminded him of them. Pa's hat hung by the front door, the one that he wore with his Sunday best. He also saw his mother's vanity mirror sitting on a unit along with some hair pins and slides. There were lots of odd things lying around that reminded him of them both and the sense of abandonment was starting to hit him. John tried to be brave, as boys try to be at that age, but he couldn't stop the tears from welling up in the corners of his eyes again. He absently wiped them away and tried to focus on making sure that he had what he needed.

As they were leaving the house, John sat in his barrow as Lucy wheeled him along. He looked back hoping that his parents would simply just walk around the corner, but when it was obvious that it wasn't going to happen, he began to wonder if he would ever see them again.

Where could they be? John thought to himself.

***

The cellar was dark and dank. The dripping of water could be heard which formed stagnant puddles on the cold stone floor. Owen woke up shivering from
the cold, despite the raging heat that his body was producing. The fever was gripping him and he genuinely thought that he might die. He had lost track of time since the day he had collected the bull from Lady Barton. He remembered vaguely going to the tavern for a drink and remembered being dragged out by Mary.

'Poor sweet Mary,' he said out loud to no one.

'She'll be worried sick. I suppose that's what comes from marrying a dreamer! If you don't have a dream how can you have a dream come true!'

He began to laugh to himself, but it hurt his head to do so.

He regathered his thoughts. He remembered collecting the bull, leading it through the town, and securing it at the bull ring. He vaguely remembered feeling tired and laying down on the hay by the bull.

'That's mine!'

He laughed again to himself, but then began to well up with tears.

'How can they do such a thing? Set the dog on the bull? What is this, the dark ages?' he said angrily.

'Then again better the dog than rats!'

He vaguely remembered the rats attacking the bull. He also remembered trying to scare them and kick them away but to no avail. He remembered the great chunks of flesh being torn from the bull. He even remembered flesh being torn off his leg by a particularly large rat.

'That rat has been eating his greens!' he laughed. 'That or his Pa is a bulldog!

His mind felt like it was moving at a hundred miles an hour.

He was reminded for no particular reason of his pet dog growing up.

'Poor Charlie!'

Owen began to sob.

'The best friend a man could ever have! You be with the angels now my sweet boy. Pa will be with you soon, and we'll go for a run like the good old days.'

He wiped his tears away with the palm of his hand.

He regathered his thoughts again and tried to remember what had happened after being attacked by the large rat. He vaguely remembered staggering away and heading to the nearest watchtower. He wanted to raise the alarm. His memory of that evening was beginning to flee his mind, and so he stopped trying to recall what happened.

Owen was feeling dreadful in every sense of the word. The bites on his legs were seriously infected and smelt of death. He would have tried to get help but he had no energy to move, not even enough to shout out. He wanted to try to move but felt something around his ankle. He looked and saw that he was chained to a nearby wooden support pillar.

He licked at a puddle of dirty water near his head and began to feel the shivers coming again. He desperately wanted to call out but began to feel dizzy and lightheaded. He passed out, thinking of his childhood dog, Charlie.

Owen's dreams were fleeting and terrifying.

In one dream, he dreamt that death was conversing with him. He was sitting with the hooded figure at a tavern bar drinking. The figure of death was exposing all of Owen's sins, and darkest secrets, to all the patrons. Owen pleaded for forgiveness from death and to give him another chance.

His dream changed and he felt his body begin to float. His body was lifted high above the town. Owen could see the townsfolk. They looked very much like ants moving about around the town. He was lifted higher and saw the Wyght island from a bird's-eye view. It was shaped like an eye and was absolutely beautiful. Owen felt at peace.

The dream shifted again and he was back at home sitting at the kitchen table with his family. Food and drink were laid out before them all. The family, however, were as still as statues, frozen in time. The family was all staring at him. He began to lose control of his bladder and urinated down one of his trouser legs.

Owen was whisked away again to the bull at the bull ring, but the bull was alive. He began to feel hungry and so attacked the bull. He bit at the bull, ripping great chunks of flesh from the beast with his teeth. The bull roared in pain and hitched its back legs trying to escape Owen's bloodied jaws. Owen laughed manically as he killed and fed on the flesh of the beast.

Owen was awoken sometime later. His head was lifted and a drink was forced into his mouth. Owen swallowed the vile liquid. It had the texture of churned-up insects and tasted like it too.

'You cannot die yet my friend,' came a voice full of hatred and venom. 'You are worth more to me alive than dead.'

Owen did not recognise the voice. The fever had dulled his senses to such a degree that he could not ascertain if the voice were even male or female. Owen felt a burning in the pit of his stomach. He felt nauseous and his head swam with dizziness. He thought that he might vomit, but the feeling passed after a few minutes. Amidst the swirling of his head, he saw the figure leave and heard the closing of what he thought was a door. His legs were still in dreadful pain but he could feel that something had been wrapped around his wounds. Owen tried to sit up but the pain gripped him again and he passed out.

Again his dreams were fleeting and terrifying.

CHAPTER 9

THE CAPTAIN & THOMAS

Captain Campion stepped off the gangplank of the ship onto the Haven docks. His long open coat flapped in the wind. In one hand he held a stout, leather bag, and in the other a black walking stick. He straightened his bushy moustache as he looked about the dock. The Captain's bowler hat raised a few eyebrows from the various folk and guards milling about, but no one approached him. He sucked on a lungful of smoke from the pipe protruding from his mouth. Another man approached from behind and stood next to him. He too wore a bowler hat and carried a bag, but this man was years younger.

'What a dump!' said the younger man.

'Now, now, Carruthers. We've only just arrived!'

'Sorry Captain,' Carruthers replied.

The dock was a mess. The road and walkways were muddy, and litter was strewn about. There were sailors and dock workers about, all working at loading and unloading cargo while trying to avoid the rats that were constantly getting under their feet. The Captain saw a large number of guards around the docks. No doubt this was a key place that needed to be guarded.

The Captain also saw several prostitutes talking to sailors. The sight of them disgusted Captain Campion. His training in his Majesty's regiment, and then the police force, and then in detective work, always kicked in when he saw those that sailed close to the edge of the law. His love of

God also caused him to be repulsed by brazen, sinful conduct. He tried to not pass judgement and to focus on the reason he and Carruthers were sent there.

They were there to investigate the disappearance of a man and his wife. The disappearance of a married couple was hardly a reason for a Constable and Sargent to be sent all the way from London, but the Wyght island inhabitants were not your usual type of people. Captain Campion questioned whether many that lived here even knew the truth of the island. Some maybe, he assumed, but probably not many. Not even Sargent Carruthers was privy to that classified information, not many were.

The men needed to get to the town of Brading. The Captain saw a carriage with an old man sitting at the helm eating an apple, so approached him.

'Good day to you sir,' called the Captain. 'Would you be able to take us to Brading?'

Captain Campion tossed a silver coin up to the man who caught it and quickly tucked it into his pocket.

'No problem squire,' replied the man with a mouthful of apple. 'Hop in. It's only a few minutes away.'

'Thank you, kind sir,' the Captain replied.

At that, he opened the door to the carriage and the two men got in.

The trip to Brading was short and uneventful. The Captain noted that the town was located on a hill surrounded by a beautiful landscape. Its close proximity to the harbour made it a key town on the island.

'I know we've talked about this Captain, but I still don't understand. Why are we here for just a simple missing persons case? Surely it's a job for the local guard!'

'Normally you would be right Sargent, but ours is not to question why. We are to simply follow our mandate.'

'Yes, I know! It is strange though.'

Matthew Ryan

As the carriage arrived in town, the Captain noted a large number of rats. Carruthers spotted them too.

'They have a serious rat problem here. We'll need to watch out. One bite from them could end our trip real quick!' complained Carruthers.

'They have about as much interest in you, as that lady had whom you were flirting with back in Portsmouth!'

'Steady now Captain,' retorted Carruthers. 'She smiled at me! She even touched my arm!'

Captain Campion raised an eyebrow cynically.

The carriage came to a halt outside the Kyngs Arms tavern. The two men got out and gave their thanks to the driver of the carriage. Captain Campion reached into a pocket and pulled out some papers. He looked at one which appeared to be a map and began to walk further into the town followed closely by Carruthers. The townsfolk gave them curious glances but no one dared to approach the two men. They arrived outside the town hall but took a small path that led to the rear of the town hall and the church. There was a building where a guard was at his post outside. The building was called "Gunne House".

'Good day sir,' said the Captain to the guard. 'We are here to see the Mayor, Lord Mulberry.'

'Yes sirs, please step inside,' the guard replied.

As the two men entered, the guard stepped in and closed the doors. He then led them through the main hall, up a set of stairs, and into an office where Lord Mulberry was sitting. Upon seeing the two men Lord Mulberry stood.

'Welcome! I'm the Mayor, Lord Mulberry. Can I help you, gentlemen?'

The guard turned and left.

'It is good to meet you, my Lord! My name is Captain Campion and this is my assistant, Sargent Carruthers. I am the Constable that has been assigned to look into your missing persons case.'

'Constable?' said the Mayor. 'I haven't requested an
and I can take care of the situation.'

'I'm afraid not my Lord. The Brotherhood sent a lette
involvement. It was signed by Brother Dhillon himself!'

The Mayor's face dropped.

'He also said in his letter,' continued the Captain. 'That I should request a meeting with Sister Agatha if there were any problems. I believe she overseers this jurisdiction.'

The sound of Sister Agatha's name turned the Mayor's face pale. The Captain handed the letter to the Mayor who quickly looked over it.

'Yes,' said the Mayor. 'This seems to be in order. It's good to meet you. I'm so glad you're both here. Please, take a seat!'

Lord Mulberry motioned for them to sit.

'I must ask,' began the Mayor. 'Are you The Captain Campion? Captain "Conquest" Campion?'

'Yes, but that was a long time ago my Lord.'

'Your reputation is well known! I'm sure you'll be a great help in solving this case.'

Captain Campion looked about the small room and saw shelves of books and trinkets. The room was cluttered and messy apart from the table where the Mayor sat. It simply had some documents, an inkwell, and a burned-out candle. There was also a flagon of ale which the Mayor drank from.

'Can I get you, gentlemen, a drink? I'm sure you are both thirsty after your long journey.'

'No need my Lord. We will check into the tavern shortly to rest up and will proceed with our investigation tomorrow morning. Have there been any further developments in the last few days?

'No!' replied Lord Mulberry. 'The guards have conducted general searches, but a more thorough search will be needed.'

'Of course,' replied the Captain. 'I will speak to the family tomorrow pefully, the case will be resolved quickly. We'll update you as the estigation continues. We'll check into the tavern now, with your leave my Lord.'

'Of course,' interjected Lord Mulberry.

The two men thanked the Mayor and left the room, leaving the Mayor looking extremely agitated.

***

Things had gone downhill for aunt Emmy and uncle Rupert since the disappearance of Thomas's parents the week before. Aunt Emmy was avoided by others in the town, and Uncle Rupert had lost a lot of work. In fact, he had lost so much work that Thomas was no longer required.

Thomas had gone to the only person he knew that may give him work, Mr Cooper the owner of the tavern. Mr Cooper was thrilled with the prospect of having a young man help him and immediately put Thomas to work. Within hours of being hired, Thomas had learned so much. He had learned how to change barrels and repair bar stools, and even how to pour a perfect pint. By the end of his first shift in the tavern, he wanted to own a tavern himself. Thomas had even contemplated names for his tavern such as "The Iron Man," or "The Dark Knight."

On this particular day, Thomas was emptying the rat traps. The traps he noted, were needing to be emptied more regularly each day. Thomas had just worked on the traps in the cellar and so began to head upstairs to work on the ones in the guest rooms.

He opened the door to the first room to find a pistol pointing at his face. He dropped his bucket which contained around a dozen dead rats and backed away.

'I'm sorry lad but you didn't knock. I was just cleaning my pistol,' said the man with the moustache.

Thomas saw that it was just the barrel of the pistol pointing at him and that the man was cleaning it out with a small, thin brush. The other parts of the pistol were spread out on the table.

'I'm sorry sir,' said Thomas a little shaken. 'I didn't realise we had guests staying in this room.'

'Don't worry lad, we only arrived earlier this morning. My name is Captain Campion.'

'It's good to meet you, sir. My name is Thomas.'

The two shook hands.

'My assistant is staying in the next room. You may want to knock before going in there,' said the Captain smiling.

'I will sir,' said Thomas a bit more at ease. 'We don't really get many staying at the tavern, well, not since I've been working here. It's probably because of the rats. You here on business or for pleasure?'

'Business I'm afraid Thomas, I'm a Constable from London. I've been assigned to investigate the disappearance of a married couple.'

'My Ma and Pa?' asked Thomas enthusiastically.

'Mr and Mrs Smith. Are those your parents?'

'Yes! I'm so glad you're here. We are all worried sick about them. Pa has gone missing for a few days before, but Ma has never left us for even one night! We're all worried that something terrible has happened!'

'Well, we're here to investigate the case. We will arrange for thorough searches to be done and also for door-to-door inquiries to be made. I'm sure your parents will be found alive and well. I would very much like to speak to you and your other family members. Could you tell me where you live so that we can pop by, maybe tomorrow morning, to speak to you and your family more formally?

'Of course Captain. I'll let the others know. I'll write our address down for you.'

'Thank you, Thomas,' replied the Captain.

CHAPTER 10

LUCY & JOHN

The Constable and his assistant had arrived as planned the very next morning. The two men entered aunt Emmy's and uncle Rupert's home and introduced themselves. Lucy was still feeling on edge about the rats but was more concerned about her parents. The Constable asked questions while the Sargent noted down the relevant information. He asked about her Ma and Pa and the kind of people they were. They also asked for information about the family, the town, and also any associates or enemies they may have. Lucy didn't like this questioning. To her, it felt irrelevant. She felt that they were wasting time and that they should be out looking for her parents, instead of just asking questions. The two men gave reassurances about finding her parents, but it did little to ease the knot that had been tying in her stomach since the day she had last seen them.

After the two men had gone, everyone had gone out leaving Lucy in the home alone. Lucy felt frustrated and useless. She hated the fact that she was scared of the rats. Before the incident by the river, she had believed that she was afraid of nothing. She believed that she could do anything that she put her mind to, but here she was crippled by her new fear. She did muster up boldness and look in town when her folks had first gone missing, but again she became terrified after the encounter with the rat outside the tavern. Her fear was so bad that she had not been out of the house since.

Lucy paced backward and forwards in the small kitchen trying to muster up the courage to step outside again. She needed to face her fear and move past it. She knew she needed to do it in order to help find her parents. She thought of John who had just returned to school after having several days off. He couldn't walk but he still managed to face his trials and difficulties. He was brave in the face of danger. He was courageous, just like she used to be. Lucy needed courage again and began to think of ways that she could get it back.

***

John had returned to school following the disappearance of his parents to a slightly more sympathetic Mrs Grisham. When he entered normally, she would give him a customary greeting and then leave him and his friends alone until the end of the day. Today, however, was different. When John entered on his barrow pushed by Uncle Rupert, Mrs Grisham strangely enough was extra happy and helped John out of his barrow herself. She also told John to ask her if he needed anything. Even when Will and Alice joined him she still came over now and then to check on him.

On one particular occasion when she had asked if John needed anything, Will spoke up.

'Why is she being so nice to you John?'

'I'm not sure,' he replied.

Alice wrote down a question.

'I think you're right Alice. It probably is because my folks are missing,' said John.

'It's also probably because she has a guilty conscience!' said Will.

'What do you mean?'

'She probably played a part in their disappearance!'

'Don't joke about such things Will,' said John a little annoyed.

'You ever seen her coming and going from her house on the edge of town? She always acts very suspiciously!'

'No, I've never even seen her outside of school, anyway, how the heck have you seen her?'

'My Ma and Pa told me! They say she wraps herself in a cloak with a deep hood and avoids other people! She always sticks to the shadows and alleyways and avoids contact with others on the street. They said that if it were the dark ages, she'd get tried for being a witch!'

'I think your parents are trying to scare you!'

Alice tugged John's arm showing him what she wrote.

'Alice said that her house is very creepy looking.' said John.

'See! Maybe she is a witch!' said Will.

John had never heard anything so ridiculous, but the woman was acting very odd. John looked over at her and she smiled back at him.

Yes, she is acting very suspiciously, thought John.

CHAPTER 11

THOMAS & OWEN

It had been a week since Thomas and his siblings had relocated to aunt Emmy's house. More searches for his parents had been carried out, but there had been no success in finding either of them. The rat infestation in Brading, however, was getting worse. There had been a town meeting where the Mayor had agreed to hire rat catchers to try to rid the town of the vermin.

Thomas stood at the Northern entrance to the town as the first group of hired men came by. There were around a dozen others who had come to see who the first rat catchers would be. The first of the catchers entered the town on a wagon. There were three men.

The first man on the wagon was a grizzled old man with a moustache and grey hair. He looked as though he had fought in the Hundred Year's War, and won it by himself. He looked as tough as old boots. He was the one who was in control of the reigns. He dipped his hat at the group of people gathered at the entrance, as they rolled past.

The second person on the wagon was a middle-aged man who had a very serious look about him. His hair was receding and he wore eyeglasses. He appeared to be talking angrily to the third man on the wagon.

The third man was in his early twenties. He had ginger hair and a ginger beard and was wiry in his build. He was tending to a net as the cart rolled on by and was nodding in response to the other man who was continually moaning at him.

Thomas watched as the wagon continued through the town heading up the Main Street toward the town hall. Thomas was so preoccupied with the hired men that he didn't notice the young lady approach.

'You not going to say hello?' she asked.

Thomas turned and to his surprise, it was the beautiful girl he had seen the day of Monty's death.

'Don't tell me,' she said. 'You were counting chickens!'

Thomas laughed. A sound that had not come out of his mouth in such a long time now.

'Not quite,' he replied bashfully.

'I'm so sorry to hear about your folks. Still no news about your mother or father?'

'None.'

'You know what you need, don't you?'

'What?'

'You need a distraction,' she said while playing with a lock of her long hair.

'What did you have in mind?'

'I'm sure I could find something to keep you busy,' she laughed. 'Let's go for a walk.'

The two began to walk eastward toward the Haven docks through a field. The girl's name he learned was Molly. She had long flowing blonde hair that was braided in several places that waved gently in the breeze. The most remarkable thing Thomas noted about her were her eyes. They were eyes you could get lost looking into. Thomas would fight roaring lions for a look into those eyes.

Thomas learned that Molly was born in Brading. Her father and stepmother owned the farm to the South and she had no siblings. There was a brother and sister born after Molly, but neither had lived for more than a few days. Molly was relieved that there were no other children in her family. No child should have to grow up in a world like this she had explained. She hated the town, and she hated her life.

The two reached the top of a large hill that looked down on the Haven docks. The sun was shining and the birds were singing. It was a moment of true beauty that Thomas vowed never to forget. As they stood at the top of the hill, Molly took Thomas' hand and held onto it with hers.

'I get scared up on the hills,' she whispered gently.

'Why?' asked Thomas.

'Sometimes I feel that I'll get blown away by a gust of wind.'

Thomas put his arm around her waist and held her close. She leaned her head on his shoulder and the two stood for a moment in silence.

'What are you thinking about?' she asked.

'I'm thinking that I don't want this moment to end,' he replied softly.

She lifted her head and turned to face him. He looked into her gorgeous eyes feeling dumbstruck. She reached up on her toes and gently brushed her lips against his. At that moment Thomas felt elated. He held her waist and she put her arms around his neck and they kissed again. Her lips were soft and tasted of honey. He didn't want the moment to end, but it did. Molly let go and stepped back.

'I should be getting back,' she said.

'Can I walk you home?'

'No, we better keep this secret for the moment. Too many gossips in this town!'

'When can I see you again?'

'Meet me under the Yar bridge tomorrow morning,' she replied.

'I'll be there!' he said excitedly.

She reached up and kissed him on the cheek and quickly ran back toward town. Thomas slumped onto the grass looking up at the clear blue sky.

What is happening? he thought to himself. *My mother and father are missing, and I'm falling in love with a girl I hardly know. I've never felt this way before! There have been girls of course but nothing like this! I've never even kissed a girl before!*

Thomas just lay on the grass thinking of Molly. Nothing else entered his mind and nothing else mattered.

Thomas arrived home an hour later to find everyone sitting at the kitchen
table eating. Thomas joined them. As he sat he took a small bread roll and ate at it absently. The talk at the table was about the rat catchers. They talked of the three that Thomas saw arrive, but more arrived after that. Apparently, a well-dressed man rode in on a stallion with an assortment of equipment and tools attached to the saddle. Another group followed on a wagon that were all women. There was even an individual who was a priest. Thomas didn't pay much attention. He simply thought about his beloved Molly and the kiss they shared. The whereabouts of his parents was currently absent from his mind.

***

A rat brushed past Owen's face causing him to wake up. His head was thumping but it felt as if his fever had broken. He no longer felt that he was on the verge of death, although he still felt light-headed and sick. Looking about Owen could see about a dozen rats in various places in what appeared to be a cellar. Some were grooming themselves while others were simply passing through to go deeper into the dark room. He noticed several rats eating grain from a torn sack. Owen's stomach groaned in response to seeing the grain. He was extremely hungry and so tried to shuffle toward it, but the chain around his leg restricted him.

'That grain is not for you my friend.'

The voice came from the darkest part of the cellar.

'That be for the children.'

Owen couldn't see the person who was speaking and couldn't distinguish the voice.

'Who are you?' asked Owen.

'Who I am is of no concern to you. I am simply the one who will collect the reward.'

'The reward? What are you talking about?'

'You are worth a lot of money and soon I will deliver you for payment.'

'You must have me mistaken for someone else. I'm a simple blacksmith!'

'I know exactly who you are, and I know exactly what you're worth. I'm just waiting for the price on your head to be pronounced and then I will take you from my humble abode to your new home, prison!' said the unseen figure.

'Please let me go! I beg of you! I'll pay you whatever you want!'

'Save your breath and your energy, Mr Smith. You'll need it in the next few days, I promise you.'

Owen began to sob quietly to himself.

'You rest Mr Smith and I'll see you soon.'

'Please! Let me go! I have a family! Please!'

A door shut in the darkest part of the cellar and Owen felt frightened, confused, and alone.

CHAPTER 12

LUCY & THE CAPTAIN

Lucy opened the door to see the Captain and his assistant standing there. It was dark outside and despite the light rain in the air, the two men had their hats in their hands.

'My name is Captain Campion and this is my assistant Sargent Carruthers, we met you and your family about a week ago. May we come in young Miss?'

'Of course,' answered Lucy.

She stepped away from the door and allowed the men to enter.

'Who is it?' called out aunt Emmy.

'It's the Captain and his assistant,' called back Lucy.

'Bring them through Lucy.'

Lucy showed the two men through to the main room where the family was. The room was cosy and had a fire burning in the heath. Aunt Emmy and uncle Rupert were both sitting in high back chairs near the fire. Aunt Emmy was sewing and uncle Rupert was lighting his pipe. John was sitting on a scattering of cushions in one corner reading a thick leather-bound book under candlelight. Lucy went and sat next to him. Aunt Emmy motioned to two empty chairs for the two men to sit. The two men sat and the Captain took a few deep puffs from the pipe in his mouth.

'Is Master Thomas not here this evening?' asked the Captain.

'No,' replied uncle Rupert. 'He's working at the Kyngs Arms this evening. How can we help you two gentlemen? Is there any news on our nephew or his wife?'

'Yes, and I'm afraid it is sad news,' began the Captain. 'We found the body of a woman matching the description of Mary Smith.'

At that moment, Lucy felt as if her whole world had been torn apart. John began to cry and nuzzle into Lucy's shoulder.

'I know this has come as a shock to you all but please be assured that we will not rest until this case is resolved.' said the Constable.

'Do we know if it was an accident?' asked Uncle Rupert.

'I'm afraid that we cannot say at this point.' replied the Captain.

'I can't believe it!' said aunt Emmy. 'I just can't believe it! Is it definitely her?'

'The body matches her description, but we will need someone to come with us to make a formal identification,' replied the Captain.

'I'll come,' said uncle Rupert.

'Thank you. Sargent Carruthers will take you to the undertakers.'

'I'll just get my hat and coat.'

Uncle Rupert got up out of his chair and left the room.

The Captain and his assistant stood and headed toward the front door.

'If there is anything you need please do not hesitate in contacting me or Sargent Carruthers.'

The men stepped out the front door leaving Lucy and John sobbing in each other's arms, and aunt Emmy for once in her life lost for words.

***

The discovery of Mary's body was made by Mr McGee, a local grocer who was well respected in the community. Mr McGee sat across from Captain Campion and Sargent Carruthers in the makeshift office, the two men had set up in Gunne House.

Matthew Ryan

The body had been taken to the undertakers who were located in the town of Sandown. Even though the body was mostly unrecognisable, it was clearly identified by Rupert Jones as Mary Smith. The Captain and Sargent began to question Mr McGee.

'We thank you for taking the time to speak to us Mr McGee,' began the Captain. 'We will only be brief but we just need to ascertain some details from
you about the discovery. Would you be able to tell us please how you found the body?'

'I'm a grocer,' said Mr McGee. 'I was on my way from Sandown to Lower Ryde. On route, I became tired and decided to pull my cart over at a local area just beyond Brading. I got off my cart and headed to a nearby tree where I thought I would have a quick nap before moving on. As I sat down I saw what appeared to be somebody asleep on the grass. The grass was long, so I couldn't see who it was, so I called out to the person. There was no answer and so I investigated and found the body.'

'Did you know the victim?' asked Sergeant Carruthers.

'Not very well. She had purchased groceries from me before and I was acquainted with her enough to say hello if passing, but I didn't know her or her family very well. They haven't been living in the town for very long.'

'Do you have an alibi for the day that she went missing? It was the same day as the disappearance of the Brading town bull.' asked Sargent Carruthers.

'Yes, I was in the Kyngs Arms with several of the townsfolk who I'm sure would be able to vouch for my whereabouts.'

'We thank you for your time,' said the Captain. 'Feel free to leave and if you have any other information please do not hesitate in letting us know.'

At that, Mr McGee stood and left the room.

'Give me your thoughts Carruthers!' asked the Captain.

'It's a very strange one, sir. The coroner's report clearly confirms that she was murdered, and the only one who doesn't have an alibi is her husband who is still missing. Logically it would appear that he murdered his wife and then fled the scene. After all, they did have an altercation in the tavern in front of the patrons. That is surely proof enough!'

'That is very logical reasoning Carruthers but let me ask you this, why did Mr Smith take the town bull?'

'Maybe he took the bull in order to sell it so that he could fund an escape from the island.'

'Again good reasoning Carruthers, but the bull was dead! How could he have moved it? Do you think the missing bull is even linked to the disappearance of Mr Smith?'

'Probably not. We only have the statement made by Lord Mulberry to say that he was involved in the disappearance of the bull, but I suppose the two events may not be linked at all?'

'Yes, I would agree. I am of the opinion that he may have accidentally killed his wife and then ran away to avoid punishment.'

'Possibly Captain, but why was her face missing and chunks of flesh ripped out of her body?'

'I don't think Mr Smith caused those injuries, Carruthers. I believe that those injuries were a result of the wildlife in the woods nearby. The pieces of this puzzle are slowly coming together, but we urgently need to find Mr Smith. The island is a small place and I'm sure we will catch him quickly. I have arranged for wanted posters to go up throughout the island offering a reward for his capture. Let's hope it yields results.

CHAPTER 13

JOHN & THOMAS

John sat huddled in the corner of the living room. Tears stained his dirty face. It had been a devastating evening and morning since the Captain had visited with the news. Uncle Rupert had been to identify the body and it was Ma.

John looked around the silent room. Aunt Emmy was still sat in the same chair she had been in the day the Captain and Sargent visited. She was staring deep into the dying embers of the fire in the heath. Uncle Rupert thought she had suffered a stroke at one point, but when he approached her she told him to leave her be. Uncle Rupert had gone out after that. He had said that he had things to do at the smithy and so left everyone to mourn. Lucy was asleep in one of the armchairs with a blanket wrapped around her.

Thomas had not taken the news well but was determined to be strong for the family. He had initially cuddled up with him and Lucy trying to comfort them. He then went to bed and wasn't seen again until early the next morning. Ever since getting up he had been tidying and trying to do chores around the home. He even offered to make aunt Emmy a drink and something to eat but she declined. Thomas then went over and sat with John. Thomas put his arm around him.

'How are you today little brother?'

'I'm just completely shocked and I'm really worried about Pa.'

'I'm sure he's ok. He probably got drunk and walked off, and fell into a ditch somewhere.'

'Do you think he hurt Ma?'

'Of course not! We know Pa better than anyone else in this town, and yes he can be stupid at times, but he's not a murderer!'

John thought back to what Will and Alice told him at school about Mrs Grisham.

'Do you think the schoolmistress has anything to do with this?' asked John.

'Mrs Grisham! No! Why?'

'Just something my friends were saying at school. They said that she was a witch and that she was probably the one responsible for what had happened to our family.'

'John, this is not the dark ages! There are no such things as witches!'

'I know, but they were saying that she was acting very odd. They said that she walks around in public wearing a long black cloak and hood, and always walks in the shadows like she doesn't want to be seen. They also said that her house on the edge of town was creepy!'

'They're just kids being kids. They're probably just exaggerating stories that they've heard. Pay it no mind.'

Thomas hugged John a little tighter.

'You'll look after us, won't you Thomas?'

'Of course! I always have and I always will.'

John felt a glimmer of comfort and fell asleep with John stroking his hair.

***

After John had fallen asleep, Thomas gently laid him down on the cushions they were sitting on and then got up. He checked with aunt Emmy if she needed anything, but she dismissed him with a wave of her hand. Lucy was still asleep in the armchair and uncle Rupert was at the smithy, so Thomas went to visit Molly. Molly had been a great support to him and so he longed to see her. He thought that he would surprise her where she lived.

As he walked he thought of the last few times he had met up with Molly. They would meet under the river Yar bridge and walk together several miles out of town so that they could be alone.

Molly had told him about her sad life. She had told him that she went through a traumatic experience as a child that had almost killed her, but she would tell him when the time was right. Shortly after that terrible experience her mother died and her father remarried, but her new stepmother was evil. She looked down on Molly and blamed her for being barren. She had been forced to live in the attic of the barn from the age of about thirteen. The attic itself was very homely and it had the added advantage of being difficult to access. Her stepmother couldn't climb the ladder, so it also became a safe space for Molly. Her father made sure that she was fed and regularly gave her small amounts of money to care for herself, but apart from that, she was alone.

Thomas had never been into the barn where Molly lived, but today he was going to surprise her. He approached the barn from an angle away from the farmhouse so as not to be seen, and entered through an open back doorway. The smell of straw was heavy in the air and the mounds of hay all around dwarfed him. Thomas crept in slowly and quietly. As he walked he heard scratching from nearby, and then a bucket falling and clattering on the floor.

'Molly!' Thomas called in a hushed voice. 'Are you here?'

Another clang was heard from behind one of the tallest mounds of hay. Thomas crept slowly around the haystack to see what was making the noise. As Thomas peered slowly around the haystack he was grabbed from behind and pushed straight into the pile of hay. Molly laughed and climbed on top of him kissing him passionately. He ran his fingers through her soft hair as they kissed and then Thomas said something stupid without even thinking about it.

'Will you marry me?' he said while looking into her eyes.

She kissed his forehead and replied.

'Yes! A thousand times yes!'

Thomas felt elated. He'd never even considered asking her to marry him. He had been so distracted lately with everything that had happened, but the moment had felt right. Molly slid off Thomas and slumped next to him in the hay holding his hand.

'Do you really want to marry me?' she asked.

He rolled onto his side facing her and kissed her head.

'Of course. I love you so, so much!'

'I love you too!'

The two snuggled into each other more closely.

'Where are we going to marry?' she asked.

'I heard of a place on the mainland. It's a place up North in Scotland called "The Green" I think. Apparently, young lovers run away to be married there all the time!'

'But how are we going to get there?'

'I'll make the arrangements. I'll get us passage onto a boat at the Havens and we'll go from there. You ok leaving your Pa?'

'Yes, what about you? Could you honestly leave your family, especially with everything that is happening?'

'If possible I'd like to take Lucy and John with us if you didn't mind.'

'Of course, we'll be one happy family.'

The two kissed and then lay in each other's arms.

CHAPTER 14

OWEN & THE CAPTAIN

Owen awoke feeling a cold breeze against his face and body. His head thumped rhythmically and a bright light blinded him as he tried to open his eyes. His fever had returned again over the last few days in the cellar, and Owen had been drifting in and out of consciousness ever since. The unknown stranger had forced the vile liquid into his mouth every time he awoke. The liquid did not help him to recover, but at least he was still alive.
His dreams had continued to be terrifying and fleeting during his unconscious state and what he remembered of them deeply disturbed him.

This day, however, was different. Owen had felt himself being carried out of the cellar he had been kept in, and out into the bright light of day where he felt the bitter wind against his body. He hadn't felt the wind or seen the sun for what felt like forever. He managed to open his eyes against the bright light of the sun to see that he was being carried across a stable yard. He was then laid upon an open-backed cart and chained to a post in the middle of the cart. The unknown stranger then mounted the cart, picked up the stirrups, and then motioned for an unseen horse to start moving.

As the cart made its way along, Owen could see the familiar sights of the houses of Brading. His immediate thought was that he had been held captive in the town itself. He may even know his captor, but Owen had been unable to see the person's face and hadn't been able to discern the voice. As the cart trundled through town Owen saw the smithy. It was closed up but smoke rose from its chimney. As they passed other buildings he noticed they were locked and boarded up too. There was no one even on the street and it struck him as odd. Owen managed to work his way toward the edge of the cart and looked down at the road. There were hundreds of rats moving up and down the street.

What the heck is going on! he thought to himself.

As they passed other buildings he saw people looking out their windows at him, but Owen couldn't see who they were. He may have known them all, or possibly even none of them. The cart came to a stop outside the town hall where the unknown figure dismounted and strode in through the town hall doors. Owen glanced around and could still see no one on the street.

The town hall doors opened. Lord Mulberry walked out followed by four guards and two men in bowler hats. The unknown figure was behind the group but kept their hood down obscuring most of their face. Lord Mulberry dropped a bag of coins into the unknown person's hands and dismissed them. Lord Mulberry then approached Owen and struck him across the face with the back of his hand.

'You thought you could escape justice Mr Smith, but justice has caught up with you!'

'Please help me!' pleaded Owen. 'I've been held captive for many, many days and I'm sick with the fever.'

'Shut your mouth scum!' shouted Lord Mulberry. 'The only help you'll be getting is help to be taken from that cart to the stocks! Guards seize him!'

The four guards moved and grabbed hold of Owen. He was unchained and lifted from the cart, and then carried to the lockup below the town hall.

The lockup was a small stone room with one window with iron bars.

The window was high up so that the prisoner could not see out without difficulty. There was a simple sleeping pallet to one side of the lockup, and in the middle of the lockup were the infamous five hole stocks. Owen was placed with his head and wrists in the contraption, and then the guards left.

Owen called out to no avail. Rats were scurrying in and out of the lockup through the window but left him alone. Owen began to question himself, wondering what he could have done to land himself in this predicament. It was shortly after this that he was informed.

***

Owen was sat at a worn oak table, with his hands and feet in fetters, when the Captain and his assistant walked in. The Captain could smell the scent of death in the air radiating from Owen. The man looked as bad as he smelt. He looked as if he had been through a session on the town whipping post.

A rat scurried across the table paying no attention to the two men or Owen. Owen knocked it away and drank a deep mouthful of water from the cracked flagon in front of him.

'This water makes a refreshing change from the mouthfuls of stagnant water I've had to endure of late!' said Owen.

'I'm glad you approve. My name is Captain Campion and this is my assistant Sargent Carruthers. I'm the Constable assigned to look into your case.'

The Captain sat down, lit his pipe, and took a few deep puffs while looking at Owen. The Sargent sat next to the Captain and looked through a few papers that he had in his hands.

'I appreciate your taking the time to speak with us Mr Smith,' said the

Captain.

'I didn't exactly get a choice!'

'You have been made aware that you are under arrest for the murder of your wife, Mary Smith. Do you have anything to say on the charge against you?'

'It's complete nonsense! Why on earth would I want to murder my wife!'

'You tell us, Mr Smith,' said Carruthers.

'I love my wife more than you could possibly know. I'd do anything for her! Ask anyone!'

'We did,' replied Carruthers. 'Apparently, she made a mockery of you in the tavern shortly before she went missing. Maybe you got angry with her and decided to shut her up.'

'Ridiculous! I could barely walk straight let alone kill anyone!'

'Let's go over the events of the day in question,' said the Captain. 'Tell us what happened.'

'My recollection is slightly hazy.'

'Convenient!' said Carruthers.

'I actually find it, inconvenient sir, especially in light of the allegations against me.'

'Tell us what you remember,' said the Captain.

'That day, the townsfolk were preparing for the festival that was to be held the next day. Most of the women and children were involved in putting up decorations, which was what I think my Mary was doing. I remember that I was working at the smithy with my uncle trying to get some work finished so that we could have the day off for the festival. We finished around midday I believe, and so I decided to go for a pint at the Kyngs Arms. After that, it starts to fade.'

'Well so far your story matches the reports we have about your movements,' said the Captain. 'What can you remember next?'

'I remember walking to Lady Barton's to collect the bull for the festival. It was a long walk and I remember that it helped me to sober up a bit.'

'You don't remember the altercation with your wife in the tavern or outside of it?' asked Carruthers.

'No, don't remember anything like that. The last I remember seeing of Mary was before I went to work that day.'

'What happened after you collected the bull from Lady Barton?' asked the Captain.

'I remember walking it back to town. I remember chaining it to the bull ring and I remember going back to the Kyngs Arms for another drink.'

'Are you absolutely sure you went back to the tavern?' asked the Captain.

'Definitely!'

'Where did you go after?'

'I don't remember!'

'Do you have any other recollections?' asked Carruthers.

'The only other thing I remember was getting bitten by something, I think it was a rat. And I remember drinking something that was like tar while being chained up in what I believe was a cellar.'

'Can you think of anyone who would want to harm you or your wife?' asked the Captain.

'No, we've only been in this town a few months. Why would anyone want to harm us?'

'I'm not sure Mr Smith,' replied the Captain.

'Any news on when I can go home?'

'Mr Smith, you are being held on suspicion of murder! You will not be going anywhere until this investigation is complete!'

Sargent Carruthers called for the guards, who came and took Owen away.

'So what do you think?' asked Carruthers.

'There are holes in his story, and in the claims about his relationship with his wife!'

'The holes in the story seem apparent, but what do you mean about his relationship with his wife?'

'Mr Smith stated that he'd do anything for his wife, but he wouldn't give up the drink for her, in fact, he went out of his way to keep it from her. There are also a few other points but I'll think about those in the coming days. I want to ascertain whether he returned to the tavern after delivering the bull to the bull ring. That will help in narrowing down the timeframe of the murder. I'll leave that to you, Carruthers. See what you can find out.'

'Yes Sir.'

CHAPTER 15

LUCY & JOHN

Lucy had a cunning plan. She was scared of the rats, she could even openly admit that, but she needed a way to deal with it. At first, she had resigned herself to staying in the house, but the rats kept getting in through the windows and various holes in the walls. She then tried to isolate herself in a single room, but again the rats found a way to get in. She even tried on one occasion to take refuge on the roof, but to her annoyance, the rats were even there.

Lucy knew that if she wanted to be kept safe from the rats then she would need to learn to deal with them, and that's when she came up with her cunning plan. She was going to learn the ways of a rat catcher, and so she befriended one of the groups that had been hired by the Mayor.

She befriended the group that consisted of the older man, the middle-aged man, and the young man. She particularly bonded with the older man with the moustache. His name was Clint and he had been a rat catcher all his life. He was a burly man who certainly knew his stuff. He taught her how to lay traps and what types of poison to use in certain situations. He taught her how to net the rats and how to dispose of the bodies. He also taught her how to defend against a rat attack and the best way to kill them.

The Middle aged man, named Brady, was very stern and everything seemed to frustrate him. Brady was different when it came to Lucy though. He was always kind and patient with her. He treated her completely different from the younger man. Lucy had seen Brady wallop the younger man across the head several times for doing things wrong, but the younger man simply took the abuse.

The younger man was called Hopper. He was very knowledgeable but not very practical. He knew absolutely everything but was pretty useless, especially at catching rats. He mostly repaired things and carried out other menial tasks for the other two men. One thing Lucy did learn about the younger man was that he could run. Lucy had seen Hopper several times running around doing errands and such, but the speed that he could run was jaw-dropping.

Lucy spent about a week with the three men learning from them and working with them. Despite the large number of rats caught, they were still breeding and spreading rapidly to the frustration of the group. On one particular day, they had worked in the cellar of the Kyngs Arms and had caught about twenty rats. The next day they returned and there were about fifty. Also, over the past week, the number of rat attacks had increased. More livestock was found dead and also the cats and dogs of the village had completely disappeared.

Lucy found it very strange, and Clint even more so, until the day the answer was found.

Clint and Brady were working at the property of Lady Barton. They were laying traps and placing poisons down in one of her many gardens. The plan was to set everything up and return the next day to see what the results were.

As the two men finished they returned to their wagon where Lucy was helping Hopper unravel some rope. As the two men approached a great twang was heard from behind them. Clint and Brady looked at one another and then quickly left to investigate. They returned carrying a cage that was filled with around a dozen rats. When they looked closer, however, they saw something that sent shivers up Lucy's spine. All of the rats were of normal size and colour, but there was one rat that was different. It was big, even bigger than the ones Lucy saw that day by the river. This rat was the size of a small pig. Its fur was jet black and was longer and more coarse than the regular rats. Its teeth were longer and sharper, and its eyes were completely white. It appeared to have no pupils at all. It simply sat staring at the two men not moving an inch. It was as if it were in deep thought, planning something.

'What on earth is that thing?' said Hopper completely intrigued.

'That, Hopper, is a rat!' replied Clint.

'I ain't never seen no rat like that before!' Hopper replied.

'Nor I!' said Brady.

'No one has,' said Clint. 'Not for over a hundred years! A long time ago there was a rat infestation in Lower Saxony which claimed the lives of over a hundred people. The deaths and instances here are similar, and the appearance of this rat explains it.'

Lucy felt anxious and wanted to leave, but knew she was with the right people that would keep her safe.

'How do you deal with that type of rat, Mr Clint sir?' she asked.

'To be honest honey, I don't know. We'll take it back to our lodgings and do some tests on it. If this rat has a weakness, we'll find it!'

'Shall we pack up and get going, chief?' asked Brady.

'Yeah, let's get back! Get the horses ready Hopper!'

'Yes sir,' replied Hopper.

'You coming with us missy, or you want us to drop you home?' asked Brady.

'Can you drop me home on your way back?'

'Of course,' he replied.

Lucy helped Hopper prepare the horses while Brady and Clint secured the cage of rats, and packed away some of the other equipment. They then all mounted the cart and rode off.

***

The discovery of the large rat terrified the people of Brading. Over the next few days, more sightings of these rats were seen. The town suffered seven more deaths within 48 hours. The townsfolk were too scared to venture outside of their homes. Doors and windows were boarded up and even the merchants shut up shop to keep the vermin out.

John was at home with aunt Emmy who was working hard to keep the rats from entering the house. Uncle Rupert was at the smithy, he'd been there more and more since the death of Ma. Thomas was at the tavern working and Lucy was with the rat catchers. The house was very quiet without anyone else around, apart from the two of them.

John sat on a window sill upstairs with a small knife in his hand peeling an apple. The view outside was distressing, to say the least. He could see around a thousand rats moving up and down the main street in the pouring rain. He could even see some of the bigger ones with the pure white eyes that Lucy had told him about. They were just sitting there staring at the other rats, almost like they were in charge.

'What's happening out there?' shouted aunt Emmy from downstairs.

'It's like a river of rats. How long until they go someplace else do you think auntie?

'As soon as the rats have filled their bellies and exhausted our foodstuffs they'll probably move on.'

John looked back outside and nothing had changed. He could hear a lot of banging and clattering from downstairs where aunt Emmy was trying to keep the rats out. John then heard a great crash and the sound of wood cracking.

'Auntie! What happened?'

John then heard aunt Emmy scream.

'Auntie? Are you ok?'

There was no reply, but John could hear the sound of small skittering feet. The rats had gotten into the house.

Matthew Ryan

'Auntie! Can you hear me?'

Again, there was no response but then John saw dozens of rats enter the room he was in. The rats were sniffing around the room, biting and chewing on furniture. One rat saw John on the window sill and jumped to bite him. John was fortunately beyond reach. The other rats had now also spotted John and were jumping to try to reach him too. John backed further onto the window sill trying to keep himself away from the jaws of the rats that were trying to bite him.

The rats saw that their attempts were futile so several tried to get to John in different ways. Some jumped at him from a nearby wooden chest, while others tried to climb on top of one another to reach him, but all failed. At one point, a rat got close to biting him but John threw his half-peeled apple at it and it scarpered.

John knew that it was only a matter of time before they got to him so began to look for a way to escape. More rats were entering the room and time was running out. Sweat poured down John's face as he looked out the window. It was then that he saw a way onto the roof. He knew it would be difficult, but he had to try.

He was just getting into position when he felt the pain of sharp teeth dig deep into his arm. He instinctively stabbed the rat with the small knife in his other hand. The rat screeched as it ran away but then John saw another that was almost upon him. John pocketed his knife and leaned back further on the window sill trying to get away. John's movement pushed the window open and he toppled out.

As John fell, time seemed to slow down.

He hit the floor hard feeling bones break in various places all over his body. Dizziness overcame him as he saw a swarm of rats bounding toward him. Before he blacked out, however, he saw the shape of a man dressed in black. The man was slowly walking toward him.

So death is a real person! John thought before all went dark.

PART 2

THE STRANGER

Matthew Ryan

CHAPTER 1

THOMAS & OWEN

Thomas was hard at work in the Kyngs Arms trying to stop the rats from getting in. The landlord of the tavern, Mr Cooper, had asked him to help with securing the cellar and pantry. Most of the merchants and townsfolk were at home sitting out the storm of rats and securing their properties, and the Kyngs Arms was no different. Everyone played their part in making sure the rats couldn't get in, even the serving girls.

Thomas was currently sawing wood on a table near the bar thinking of John at home with aunt Emmy.

I hope they're safe! he thought to himself as he worked. *Maybe Mr Cooper will let me leave early if I work hard.*

Thomas' thoughts were disturbed by the opening of the main door of the tavern. In the doorway stood a man dressed in black that he didn't recognise. The man was tall and wore a long black leather coat that hung at his knees. He wore dark tan boots, strange black trousers, and a white shirt open at the collar. He also wore black fingerless gloves and a leather tricorn hat. His hair could be seen and it was long and unkempt. The stranger's piercing blue eyes examined the room and its occupants.

'We're closed!' shouted Mr Cooper from behind the bar.

The stranger ignored Mr Cooper's words and pushed the door shut behind him. He then strode toward the landlord. As he walked, Thomas noticed that the man's lips held a short thin brown object that had smoke rising from the tip. The man addressed Mr Cooper who was visibly annoyed that the stranger hadn't listened to him.

'I desire a room for several nights, innkeeper!' said the man with a rough, gravelly voice.

'I said we're closed! Besides, we don't serve your kind here! I suggest you move on to the next town!'

The man reached inside his jacket. Mr Cooper stood firm but put his hand on a large butcher's knife that he kept hidden under the bar. The man pulled out a small leather bag containing coins. He then tossed the bag of coins onto the counter which produced a loud clank. As it landed several silver pieces spilled out.

Thomas had never seen so many silver coins, especially ones like these. The coins Thomas had seen before were always rough in quality and cut, but these were perfectly round and shone like the stars on a clear night sky.

'Will this suffice for your trouble innkeeper?' asked the man.

Mr Cooper picked up one of the coins, examined it, and then bit onto it. His eyes glowed with approval. He immediately picked up the bag and the other coins and pocketed them quickly.

'Of course sir. I'm sorry for my rash behaviour. Many bad folks about and the world is a changed place!' Mr Cooper replied nervously.

The man simply stared at him.

'Your room is at the top of the stairs, the last door to the right.'

'I expect food with my room!' said the man as he strode toward the stairs.

'Of course kind sir, I'll get one of the girls right on to it. I'm sorry, I didn't get your name.'

'I didn't give it!' replied the man as he climbed the stairs to his room.

Mr Cooper looked at the man suspiciously as he went and remained silent until he heard the guest enter the room and close the door. Mr Cooper turned to Thomas.

'Did you see that man? He was the strangest looking chap I've ever seen.

'Who is he?' asked Thomas.

'I have no idea but I'm going to have to keep an eye on him, he looks like trouble! I better arrange for some food to be prepared for him.'

After a short time, a tray laden with food and drink was placed on the bar ready to be taken to the stranger. Thomas could smell the bread and freshly cooked eggs, and especially the slices of bacon. There was a flagon of ale too, along with milk, a few wheat biscuits, and apples.

'Take the tray to our guest Dixie!' shouted Mr Cooper.

Dixie's head appeared from out the kitchen doorway.

'I'm not going near him!' she said angrily. 'Get Thomas to take it up!'

Thomas looked up from his task.

'Take the tray up, lad,' asked Mr Cooper.

Thomas stood and wiped his dirty hands on the front of his trousers.

'Sure thing Mr Cooper.'

'Tell him the bacon is of the finest cut!'

'Will do,' said Thomas.

He lifted the tray and began to climb the stairs to the stranger's room making sure he didn't drop anything from the tray. Thomas stood outside the man's door and gave two loud knocks.

'Your food is ready sir!'

The door swung open and Thomas saw the strangest thing. The man who had come into the Kyngs Arms now looked very different. He had removed his hat and coat and had tied his hair back. Thomas noticed that despite the fact he was wearing the same clothes he looked like a different person. It must have been the smile. The man had a beaming smile as he opened the door and his eyes were lit up in delight.

'Come in young man, come in,' he said enthusiastically.

'Yes sir,' said Thomas as he walked into the room apprehensively. 'I have your food! The bacon is of the finest cut!'

Matthew Ryan

Thomas saw that the man had lit a fire in the hearth and had his wet coat and hat hung in the corner. The man's boots were in front of the fire and Thomas could smell the warm leather.

'Put the tray on the table please young fella,' said the man.

Thomas followed his instructions and did so. He turned to leave when the man suddenly stopped him and shut the door.

'Come, pull up a chair. Let us break bread together.'

Thomas didn't understand what he meant but sat down regardless.

'You look like a young man with the weight of the world on your shoulders. Tell me what troubles you,' said the man empathetically.

'Begging your pardon sir,' replied Thomas nervously, 'but you don't even know me. How can you make such an assumption!'

'I have spoken too hastily and I am sorry my young friend. I have travelled the world and have seen many sights, and know the human heart better than most. The look you bear tells me of love and loss, and joy and pain.'

'It's true sir, but you wouldn't understand.'

'I understand all too well young man. I too had suffered a terrible loss and during my grief, I too had found love.'

'Who are you? Where do you come from?'

'I have been known by many names, but you may call me Sir Timerus.'

'It's good to meet you, Sir, my name is Thomas.'

'It is good to meet you too Thomas. That is a good name. One worthy of walking with the Christ.' replied Sir Timerus. 'Now to answer your second question, where do I come from? Well, I cannot be precise because I have been everywhere. I have travelled the seven seas and have even been to the New World!'

'The New World?' asked Thomas. 'Where's that?'

'Everyone will know of the New World one day, even you. You are an inquisitive young man Thomas. Let me ask you this, how long have the rats been in town?'

'About a month, but this last week has been the worst. Why?'

'Why? Because I'm here to save you all, that's why!'

'To save us all? Are you a rat catcher then?'

'Another good question! A rat catcher? A rat catcher?' Sir Timerus said musing to himself. 'I wouldn't say I'm a rat catcher as such, but I can catch rats. Rats, birds, people. I'm skilled in catching anything. Let me demonstrate!'

He stood and walked over to his coat. He fumbled around in an inside pocket
and pulled out a foot-long pipe of exquisite workmanship. It was made of wood but had metal worked into it in several places. The wood was carved in an intricate fashion and in a style unknown to Thomas. It was the strangest pipe Thomas had ever seen.

'A pipe? What's that for?' asked Thomas.

'This,' replied Sir Timerus, 'is a pipe like none you have ever seen. It produces the most beautiful of sounds that even the hardiest of beasts cannot escape. It is with this that I will rid your town of rats!'

'I'm sorry Sir, but I don't understand. How can a pipe rid the town of rats?'

'I will show you.'

Sir Timerus lifted the pipe to his lips and began to blow softly into the mouthpiece. A low-pitched sound came from the pipe, The man began to work his fingers in a curious way along the holes of the pipe. To a casual observer, it appeared as if his fingers were dancing along the stem of the wind instrument.

Thomas heard the sweet music and saw that the man was obviously well-skilled. Thomas then heard another sound. It was the sound of the scurrying of small feet. It was then that he saw the rat enter the room through a hole in the bottom of the wall next to the fireplace. The rat scurried along toward the table and began to climb the leg. Thomas fell out of his seat backward in shock. He quickly stood and watched as the rat mounted the table and moved toward Sir Timerus. The rat then simply sat on the edge of the table peering at the man as he played his tune. Thomas was awestruck and was about to speak but quickly closed his mouth again. What he saw was amazing. The rat was drawn to the music and was mesmerised by it. Sir Timerus then stopped playing the tune.

'You see! Amazing isn't it? said Sir Timerus proudly.

'Yes! I can't believe my eyes!' replied Thomas still awestruck.

The rat had now moved across the table and started nibbling at a piece of the bread from the tray of food. The man stroked the rat and scratched it behind its ears.

'So you draw the rats to you, and then what?' asked Thomas.

Sir Timerus lifted his hand and slammed a fist on the rat's head. He did so with such ferocious strength that when he lifted his fist again, the rat's skull was a mushy mess with blood, bone, and brains splattered everywhere.

'That, young Thomas is what I will do! I will kill every last one of them!'

Thomas felt vomit rushing up from his stomach but kept it down. He then began to tremble. *Who is this man?* he thought to himself.

Suddenly, a pounding came on the door.

'Are you ok in there Thomas?' came the voice of Mr Cooper. 'I heard a bang!'

'Yes, I'm fine.'

Thomas moved to the door still feeling nauseous.

'It was good to meet you, Thomas! I look forward to us becoming better acquainted!' said Sir Timerus.

Thomas opened the door and stepped out. Before he closed it he glanced back at the man. Sir Timerus was sitting at the table eating the food Thomas had brought up with him. The dead rat had been pushed onto the floor and blood had spilled from its broken body. Thomas closed the door and was met by a barrage of questions from Mr Cooper.

***

A few buildings away from the tavern, Owen had just finished eating his food. His meal had simply consisted of bread and water. Owen had been moved to a locked room in Gunne House after the rats began pouring into the lockup. A guard stood on duty just outside the door. The room itself was empty apart from a table and a single chair which he occupied and from which he had eaten and drank. The guards had told him, while he was being moved, that the town was being overrun by rats and that people were going missing. It was assumed that they had been killed or had fled for their lives.

After finishing his meal, Owen had begun to pray for the lives of his family and hoped that they were all safe. He was disturbed from his prayers by keys unlocking the door and the door opening. A guard stepped in and collected his empty plate and cup. Behind him walked another figure who entered the room. The guard then left the room and locked the door leaving Owen with the strange-looking individual.

The individual was dressed in a long coverall, the colour of deep purple, that ended just above black booted feet. The person wore long black leather gloves and wore a mask that covered their face. The mask had a large beak where the mouth would be. They also wore gold-rimmed eyeglasses over the top of the mask. The person looked like a blackbird crossed with a purple man. The sight sent a shiver up Owen's spine.

'Who are you?' asked Owen suspiciously.

'I am known as the Doctor!' replied the muffled voice.

'What do you want?'

Matthew Ryan

'You have been set up Mr Smith!'

'Tell me something I don't know!'

'I have come here with a proposition that will get you out of your predicament!'

Owen raised sceptical eyes as the Doctor approached.

CHAPTER 2

THE CAPTAIN & LUCY

The Town Hall was packed with townsfolk as the meeting began. Captain Campion stood with Sargent Carruthers along one wall at the side of the room. The Captain could see the various folk he had spoken to over the past two weeks and noted that all were visibly agitated and annoyed. Standing at the back of the hall, the Captain noted, was Thomas Smith with a younger lady.

The Captain felt sorry for Thomas. His family had appeared to have been hit hardest by the rats since the infestation began. The lad had lost his mother in death and his father was currently in custody for murdering her. The lad's young brother had also gone missing and so had his aunt too. The only family left for Thomas was his younger sister and his uncle, who had now locked himself away in his smithy with several bottles of rum, if the rumours were to be believed. It was definitely a very sad time for Thomas and the Captain felt for the lad.

The Captain looked at the Town council sitting at the front of the room behind a long table.

Lord Mulberry sat in the middle of the group in the largest chair. He was scribbling something down on a large sheet of parchment with a long black quill.

To Lord Mulberry's right sat the honourable Sir Fitzgerald, apparently a local war hero who was loved by some, but hated by most. He wore a monocle and had a thin moustache under his long thin nose. The

Captain had spoken to him on two occasions but found the man to be extremely rude and unpleasant.

Next to Sir Fitzgerald sat the reverend Nicholas whom the Captain had met a few days previously. The Captain could see the sweat pouring down the obese man's face and the remains of dinner down the front of his priestly garb.

To Lord Mulberry's left sat Lady Barton who was the picture of pure wealth. The Captain learned that the Lady looked down on everyone, and viewed anyone with a penny less than her as a peasant.

Next to her sat the Lord Asprey, Lord of the house of Nunwell. He was seldom seen in the town but liked to be involved in matters of the town council.

Lord Mulberry banged down his gavel on the table.

'Order! Order!' he shouted.

The large crowd in the small hall began to hush.

'We are here,' he began, 'to discuss the town's current rat infestation and to see how we can save our town and our livelihoods.'

The crowd remained silent.

'As you know, for the past month we have seen an increase in rat activity. This activity has increased so much that it has affected the lives of everyone here. In the past week especially, we have seen an increase in injuries and even deaths among not only our animals and livestock but also among our own townsfolk too. It has been reported, as many of you have seen for yourselves, that there is a different strain of rat that appears to be more aggressive and vicious than the others. It is significantly larger and is very distinct in how it looks and acts. Please do not engage with these rats!'

'What are we going to do about them Mayor?' shouted a bald man from the crowd.

'Please hold your questions. I'll open to you all in a moment.' Lord Mulberry replied.

'There is another issue I wish to speak of before we discuss the rats further, and that is the cause of the rat outbreak. We have ascertained that the cause is down to a certain Mr Owen Smith. As you all know, Mr Smith had initially fled the town but has now been caught. He is currently being held in custody awaiting criminal proceedings which will no doubt result in his being hung or sent to the Wyght Asylum.'

Just hearing the words "Wyght Asylum" caused the crowd to gasp. The townsfolk then began to talk among themselves.

'I've never heard of the Wyght Asylum.' whispered Sargent Carruthers. 'Why is everyone acting so strangely?'

'It's one of toughest prisons in the known world!' replied the Captain.

'Why haven't I heard of it?'

'The prison is top secret due to the criminals it has housed there. Only the islanders and top country officials are aware of the place!'

'How has that information never got out or spread from the island?'

'A good question, for another time.' replied the Captain.

Their conversation was disturbed by Lord Mulberry again calling for order.

'Before we go on,' he said. 'Are there any questions?'

Several men and women raised their hands.

'Yes Mrs Wallace?' said Lord Mulberry.

An elderly woman stood up to speak.

'How'd we know that Owen brought the rats?' she asked.

'I'm afraid Mrs Wallace that we cannot be certain, however, the facts fit the circumstances and we believe that he will confess to this in the next day or so. Regardless of this, Mr Smith was involved in the murder of his wife and the butchering of the festival bull. For these crimes at least, he will be punished!'

Mrs Wallace sat down.

Several other hands were raised.

'Mr Blanch, what is your question?

A middle age man stood and spoke.

'Is it true the ratcatchers have left town?'

'Some have,' replied Lord Mulberry. 'A few have also been found dead. Three are still working, trying to resolve the problem.'

The man sat down.

'Mr Goodwin? What is your question?' Asked Lord Mulberry.

An older man stood up.

'What are we going to do about the rats?' he asked.

'Unfortunately Mr Goodwin, there is no easy answer to that. We are planning to send for more rat catchers and will increase the reward. The Constable, Captain Campion, will also be sending for help from the mainland if the problem has not been resolved in the next few days. If this also fails then we will need to sit out the infestation until the problem dies down or goes away entirely. We are in for a hard few months.'

The Mayor's reply brought outrage from the crowd. All began shouting in anger and frustration. The Mayor began banging his gavel to quiet the crowd, but to no avail. It was during this chaos that the doors to the hall opened. The Captain looked around to see a man stride in wearing a long black leather coat and a black tricorn hat.

The man strode halfway into the hall and the crowd immediately fell silent.

'This is a private town meeting good sir,' said Lord Mulberry. 'Please leave immediately!'

'The man you have in custody is not guilty of the crimes you are holding him for!' said the stranger.

'We are investigating the matter and will hold our own council. What is it you want?' asked Lord Mulberry.

'I can solve your rat problem,' said the stranger as he pulled a thin brown object from his inside pocket. He placed the object in his mouth, lit it with a match, and then began to smoke it.

'Just like that?' said Lady Barton. 'You can solve it as simple as that?'

'Yes,' replied the man.

'If you manage to rid the town of rats, what is it that you would want as a reward?' asked the Mayor.

'Fifty pounds,' he replied.

'Fifty pounds!' said Lord Mulberry humorously. 'If you got rid of the rats we would happily give you five hundred pounds!'

'Fifty pounds is all I need,' replied the man.

'Then fifty pounds it is!' replied Lord Mulberry.

'I will rid the rats tomorrow at the break of day and will return another time for payment.'

At that, the strange man turned and strode off.

Before leaving, the Captain saw him look straight at Thomas before disappearing through the door. The Captain lit the pipe in his mouth and began to smoke it while thinking about the strange man who had promised to rid the town of the rats.

***

Being too young to attend the meeting Lucy had been left at home. The house had been a mess the day she and Thomas returned to find John and aunt Emmy missing. There was broken and chewed furniture, the foodstuffs had all been eaten, and there were rat droppings throughout. Lucy and Thomas were seriously concerned about John but hoped that aunt Emmy had taken him somewhere safe until the worst of the infestation was over.

Uncle Rupert however, had a different idea of what had happened to them. He believed that the rats had gotten to them and killed them. Since then uncle Rupert had remained mostly at the smithy getting drunk. Thomas tried on several occasions to help him but to no avail.

The home though was now safe again. Since the day John and aunt Emmy went missing, the rats hadn't been seen near the house. In fact, Thomas and Lucy saw rats that purposefully avoided the family home. It was all very confusing to them both but they used the opportunity to try to get the house straight again and to make repairs as best they could.

On the day of the town meeting, Lucy decided that instead of staying home alone she would head to see Clint, Brady, and Hopper. She had enjoyed the time she had spent with them and the training they gave her. She felt a lot more confident when facing the rats and felt more at ease when outside her home. The three rat catchers had rented a stable to the South of town when they first arrived and used it as a base of operations. Lucy knew a way to get there that would bring her into little contact with the rats and so she had left the house with a spring in her step. The journey to the ratcatcher's stable was quiet. She saw nobody, not even a child, but presumed everybody was at the town hall or safely locked up in their own homes.

After around ten minutes of walking without incident, Lucy arrived at the stable of the rat catchers. She banged on the front door to the building. There was no answer. She pressed her ear up against the door but heard no noise coming from inside. She decided that she would head into the yard and enter through the back door. She reasoned that they were probably busy in the yard, or simply couldn't hear her.

As Lucy stepped into the yard, the first thing she noticed was that the wagon and the horse were gone. Lucy assumed that the three men were out catching rats and were trying to earn their money. Lucy decided to wait inside for them and so headed toward the back door. As she walked through the yard she stepped over puddles of blood. The blood no doubt came from the rats that the men had captured and killed. There was nothing else of significance in the yard apart from some empty rat cages and several traps which were damaged or broken.

Lucy headed to the door, turned the handle, and stepped inside. The room was large and extremely untidy. It was a single room with various used furniture throughout. There were three sleeping pallets, a large table with chairs, and a large fireplace where the flames had died down to simple embers.

As Lucy entered the room more fully she noticed that the large table was covered in junk and uneaten food. It also had several papers at one end. Her reading skills were very good, her mother had taught her well. The thought of her mother filled her mind and made her feel sad, so she sat down on one of the nearby chairs to clear her mind.

After a few moments, Lucy lifted one of the pages closest to her and began to try to make out the words of the dreadful hard writing. She saw what appeared to be a description of the new strain of rats the men had caught. The creature was called a "Hamelin Rat" but Lucy had no idea why.

What is a Hamelin? she thought to herself.

The description of the rat made her spine shiver. She saw descriptions of the rat, such as its all-white eyes. "Eyes without pupils," it said. The fur of the rat was likened to the rough prickles of a porcupine, but again Lucy had no idea what that was. The teeth and nails were likened to steel though they were still bone. The size of the rat was described as being like that of a large cat. She also noticed that the writing said that the Hamelin rats were both blind and deaf. This absolutely fascinated her. How could these rats be so dangerous if they couldn't see or hear anything? It struck Lucy as remarkable.

Lucy picked up another sheet of paper. This one was a letter from a Dr Jekyll at the Wyght Asylum to Brady. She was about to read it when she noticed drawings on the other sheets of paper on the table. She put the letter down and examined the drawings. There were various drawings of the Hamelin rats. There was also a map of the town with various markings on it. Lucy presumed that the markings were the locations of rat nests or of where traps were to be put down.

As she continued to rummage through the papers her hand felt something very strange. It was something small and hairy. Lucy pulled her hand back in fear thinking it to be a rat. It didn't move. Lucy lifted the papers and saw something strange. It was a moustache, a false one. Lucy was confused and looked around the room and saw other strange things. She saw a wig, some eyeglasses, and also several identification documents with names she didn't recognise.

A dark sense of foreboding went through her mind and she decided that she had better leave, she had seen too much.

As Lucy stood to leave, the three men were standing in the doorway.

'Young Miss Lucy!' said Clint.

'I'm sorry sir, I was looking for you all and decided to wait, but I should be going now.'

'Nonsense!' said Clint. 'We have much to discuss with you, little miss.'

Lucy began to visibly shake.

'No need to be scared my dear,' said Brady smiling. 'Take a seat'

Lucy sat down hesitantly as the three men approached her.

CHAPTER 3

THE STRANGER & THOMAS

The stranger sat at the table in his room. The fire was burning away in the hearth, crackling as the various logs and pieces of the wood split. Outside the window, a few street lamps were flickering away. Despite the lamps, the dark was heavy this night.

The stranger was busy. His head was down over an object on the table that he was working on. Various tools were on the table and a loupe was gripped in the crook of his eye. Several rats were moving about the table picking at the crumbs that were scattered about from the stranger's last meal. One of the rats watched him inquisitively as he worked.

'Nearly done!' said the stranger out loud.

'Why do you insist on doing that every time?'

'Because it has to be done!'

'Does it really make any difference if you do it or not?'

'Of course it makes a difference, I wouldn't be doing it otherwise! My babies here deserve the best if they are to give of their lives for the cause!'

The stranger stroked the rat that was watching him. The rat allowed him to stroke it, even lifting its chin so that the man's fingers could reach its neck and chest. As the stranger returned to work the rat scurried away to investigate a different part of the table.

'Besides, it hasn't sounded the same since it broke.'

'Does the death of the many really justify the saving of a few?'

'Without question! The few that will be saved will be eternally grateful and
will live forever in paradise!' replied the stranger.

'But how?'

'Enough! It's done!'

The stranger lifted the pipe from the table and examined the new engraving. He rubbed his thumb over the new piece of silver that he had attached and looked at what was inscribed on it. The new piece of silver was inscribed with four letters, "WXIX". The stranger sat back relieved. His brow was wet with sweat, but nothing could contain the large grin on his face.

***

Thomas woke early before daybreak. He quickly got dressed and quietly left the house trying not to disturb Lucy who was still snoring away. As Thomas left the house he saw that the street was clear of rats, but there was a light fog over the town. Thomas quickly began to walk North heading toward the Kyngs Arms tavern. The fog was light enough not to hinder his sight and the various street lamps helped his vision a little too. As he walked along toward the town square he saw that the streets were completely devoid of life. Thomas supposed that even rats needed to sleep. There was a deathly stillness that unsettled Thomas but he pressed on regardless.

As he approached the town square he saw the figure of Molly who was waiting for him. She wore a long dirty red cape wrapped closely about her with a hood pulled down covering most of her face. As he approached she ran toward him and hugged him tightly.

'Any news on John, or your aunt?' she asked concerned.

'No, it's like they've vanished off the face of the earth!'

'Do you still think your aunt took John to safety?'

'We're still clinging onto that hope. We've asked around and searched but can't find anything to indicate what has happened to them, whether good or bad. Aunt Emmy is strong for her age and resourceful. She knows many on this island that would take her in, so she may have been forced to flee with John to somewhere safe.'

'Let's hope so,' she replied.

The two continued to walk on toward the tavern hand in hand.

'Are you ready for the most amazing thing you will ever see?' he asked.

'Yes, my love.'

Within a few minutes, the two arrived at the tavern and a few other townsfolk were already there. Some gave nods of acknowledgment while others talked quietly among themselves. Most were notably cold, rubbing their hands to keep warm.

As the sun began to rise Thomas saw several more townsfolk arrive and among them were members of the town council and the Mayor, Lord Mulberry. Thomas saw the Reverend and the Mayor talking in hushed voices, but couldn't hear what was being said.

It was at this moment that the door of the tavern opened and out came striding the stranger. The small crowd began to laugh at him. Even Thomas couldn't contain his smile. The stranger was dressed in the most ridiculous outfit that Thomas had ever seen. He wore a long, red silk gown that glittered with many bright colours. He wore long, red curly-toed boots with bells on the end, and on his head he wore a long, red hat with bells hanging from various places. As the stranger walked toward the crowd the outfit seemed to glint and glisten and the bells on his outfit rang with a soft, gentle sound.

'You look like a village idiot!' shouted a man from the crowd.

The crowd broke into more laughter.

The stranger strode through the laughing crowd into the middle of the road and took his position facing the main street. The stranger then spoke in a loud voice so that all could hear.

'You are going to see a sight beyond your wildest of dreams!'

The stranger lifted his hand, which contained an object so that all could see it. It was his pipe. Thomas recognised the pipe from when he saw it in the stranger's room in the tavern. The pipe was a strange-looking object that drew
everyone's attention away from the stranger's outfit. The stranger put the pipe to his lips but before he blew, he turned his head toward Thomas and gave a wink. This act did not go unnoticed by Lord Mulberry or the Reverend Nicholas.

The stranger softly blew into the pipe which gave a gentle sound. He then slowly began to move his fingers up and down the shaft of the pipe, fingering the holes, producing a calming melodious tune. The small crowd that surrounded the stranger remained silent and looked as if they were on tenterhooks. Thomas looked about to see if he could spot any rats moving but none came so far.

'What's supposed to happen?' whispered Molly.

'Just wait and see,' said Thomas smiling and giving her hand a squeeze.

A scream came from a nearby woman. She pointed at the tavern door where rats could be seen running toward the man with the pipe. There were several gasps and outcries from the crowd as the rats came. More rats came from nearby buildings and alleys, and the stranger continued to play his gentle tune. As the rats reached the stranger, they merely sat in front of him mesmerised. The crowd began to slowly back away in panic and even Molly became scared. Thomas gripped her hand for reassurance.

'Keep watching!' he whispered.

More rats began to appear. Some now came from the nearby fields, and various holes in the ground. Some even came from the church. Within just a few minutes around a hundred rats were sitting in front of the stranger listening to his song. Thomas noticed, however, that none of the rats that had gathered were the strange ones, the ones called the Hamelin rats.

CHAPTER 4

OWEN & THE CAPTAIN

Owen was awoken from his restless sleep by the sound of music. He was still securely located in a room in Gunne House and was still shackled by his hands and feet. The Doctor had gone but had promised to return.

Owen was shivering and his body ached. The infection that had developed while being held captive had seriously impacted his body. He was also sore around his wrists and ankles from the tightness of the shackles. He tried in vain to make his wrists more comfortable but the chains were too tight. The fresh bruises he had received from the guards after being imprisoned were particularly sore and had turned purple and black in places.

He lifted his head and tried to see out of the window to locate the source of the music, but saw nothing except the roof of the building opposite. Instead, Owen decided to think about the Doctor's proposal.

The proposition was very tempting, but he knew he would lose everything if he accepted. Owen reasoned that if he was going to go down for the crimes that he had been accused of, then he'll have no choice but to accept the Doctor's offer. He prayed, however, that it would not come to that. The Doctor had said that two choices would be put before him by the town officials, the choice of pleading guilty to the crimes or pleading not guilty. If Owen pleaded not guilty but was found guilty by the court, then he would hang. If however, Owen pleaded guilty then he would be shipped to the Wyght Island Asylum for incarceration.

At first, it seemed quite logical to Owen, he would rather live than die but there was a problem. Everyone on the island knew that to be sent to the asylum was worse than death itself. The inmates there were rumoured to be subjected to torture and experiments. You would be housed with some of the most evil and violent individuals in the world and would be at their mercy. Anyone who ever stood before officials to make this choice tended to always choose death. It was the lesser of the two evils.

The Doctor, however, wanted Owen to plead not guilty and to go to the asylum. The Doctor wanted to experiment on an individual that was not psychotically crazy. He wanted to run tests on individuals that were honest and decent like Owen so that he could further his research. The Doctor promised that Owen would be released after a year, but he was never to tell of what happened at the asylum or the tests he would be subjected to. He would need to begin a new life under a different identity.

It was a difficult decision but hoped that evidence would be found of his innocence so that he could be freed instead.

***

A few rooms down from Owen, the Captain and the Sargent stood at a window watching the events unfold in the town below. They watched as the stranger played his pipe, and as the rats began to flock to him. They then saw the stranger moving along the street, dancing and playing his pipe. The rats followed behind still entranced by the stranger and the sound of the music.

'Have you ever seen anything like it?' asked the Sargent.

'No Carruthers. I have seen various animals trained to do many tricks by the use of pipes and whistles, but nothing like this.'

'Look at his clothing. He looks like a jester and is acting like one too. Maybe that's what he is, or once was!'

'Carruthers, that outfit and the way he wears it are not normal!'

'What do you mean Captain?'

'What I mean is, is the man is not a jester. Rather he is a man trying to look and act like a jester!'

'I don't understand Captain! Whether he's a jester or is trying to act like one makes no difference!'

'It makes a world of difference Sargent.'

'But why?'

'Because my learned friend,' said the Captain. 'The reason that he acts like someone he's not is to conceal his true identity and his true intentions.'

'What are his true intentions?'

'Of that, I'm not sure, but I'm sure we will find out!'

The two men watched as the stranger continued his dancing and his pipe playing as he travelled up the street. More, and more, rats were beginning to follow him. The two men also saw a sizeable group of townsfolk following behind at a distance, all cheering and clapping. After a few moments the stranger, the rats, and the crowd, all disappeared from sight leaving the streets empty and devoid of life.

The Captain struck a match and lit his pipe. He moved to sit in a nearby worn leather chair contemplating the stranger and the other events that had happened in the town over the past few weeks.

CHAPTER 5

LUCY & THE STRANGER

Lucy chose the best spot so that she could see the events happening in the town. She had climbed old mother oak which was a tree perched on one of the higher hills on the outskirts of Brading. Old mother oak, as the tree was affectionately known, had apparently been sitting on that hill for around a thousand years, or so they claimed. Lucy had no idea how they could know such a thing, but today that didn't matter. Today, old mother oak was the means Lucy used to see the stranger and the rats.

Lucy had seen it from the very start. As soon as she noticed that Thomas had left her that morning, she got ready and left to see the spectacle for herself. When she had first climbed old mother oak, she had seen Thomas and the blonde girl waiting near the tavern with a small group of townsfolk. Lucy had seen the stranger exit the tavern in his colourful outfit and had seen the rats come as the song was played.

It was an amazing scene to behold. At first, there had been just a dozen or so of the vermin, but then it became hundreds and then thousands as the stranger continued on through the streets. It made Lucy smile looking at the stranger in his ridiculous outfit, skipping and dancing to his own song.

'Amazing, isn't it!' said a voice from below her.

Lucy almost fell out of the tree when the man had spoken.

'It's you, Mr Clint! I didn't hear you down there.'

'Ai, it's just me!' He said. 'You wanted to get a good look, eh my dearest?'

'Yes, I was intrigued.'

'That man there,' said Clint pointing at the stranger. 'He is extremely dangerous!'

'What do you mean Mr Clint sir?'

'You remember yesterday in our lodgings that I said that we were hired to do a job and that the job involved spying on someone and using disguises.'

'Yes,' she replied.

'Well, he's the job. He's the one we're spying on.'

'Him? Why?'

'He's known as the Piper and he is a wanted criminal. Everyone in the world has been hunting for him for many years.'

'What did he do?'

'He killed hundreds of children.'

The hairs on Lucy's neck stood up and she felt her blood run cold.

'How?' she asked, as she looked at the stranger.

'A long time ago, hundreds of years, in fact, a man went to a city in Lower Saxony. You know where that is?'

'No,' said Lucy.

'It doesn't matter. Anyway, the city was called Hamelin. Do you remember me showing you the Hamelin rat?'

'Yes, was the rat named after that city?'

'That's right m' dearest. The city was full of rats and no one could get rid of them. The Piper showed up with his pipe and played a song that made the rats follow him to a river, where the rats all drowned.'

'Wow!' Lucy said.

'The city Governor, however, refused to pay the Piper. The Piper then returned a short time after and played a song that drew all the children after him. They followed him to their doom!'

'What a terrible story! Why didn't the adults stop the Piper from taking the children?

'They we're all busy, distracted.' Clint replied.

'What happened to the children?'

'No one knows. He took them into a cave and they were never found again!'

'That's awful! But why do you think he's the same man? You said that event happened hundreds of years ago! Surely that man is dead by now.'

'Maybe or maybe not! Maybe he has powers, or maybe it's something to do with his pipe. You can see for yourself what he's doing!'

Lucy looked again at the stranger. The view defied belief. The man was prancing about to his song and the rats followed. They appeared to all be heading toward the river Yar.

'Maybe we should tell the Mayor, or the guards, or even the Captain!' Said Lucy.

'They're keeping an eye on him, and if he strikes they'll be ready to take him down!'

'Why don't they just arrest him now?'

'He hasn't done anything wrong yet! Not here anyway. They just need to catch him in the act of trying to take the children and then they'll arrest him!'

'I need to warn Thomas!'

'No Lucy, you mustn't tell anyone. I shouldn't have even told you!'

'Why did you?' she asked.

'Because the three of us think you're a great girl, you're almost one of the team. I also wanted you to know why we've been acting a little strange over the last few days, especially after you saw those things back at our lodging. You've been great with helping us and so I wanted you to know. You mustn't tell anyone mind you!'

'I won't,' she replied.

'Good girl!'

Matthew Ryan

***

The time was approaching that the stranger was secretly dreading. It was the moment when he would kill the rats in front of the entire town.

The stranger had skipped and danced in his merry little outfit while playing his special tune on his pipe. There were now thousands upon thousands of rats following him completely enchanted by the song. Following the rats were the townsfolk, and all had come out to watch the great spectacle. The stranger had played his tune on the main route through the town of Brading and was now nearing his destination, the river Yar bridge. The bridge was between one of the town's watchtowers and the town water mill and extended over one of the deeper parts of the river.

As the stranger reached the foot of the bridge, where the rats would die, he stopped walking and the rats stopped too. The rats were still all completely enchanted by the stranger and clung to every sound coming from his pipe.

The stranger then began to lead into a new song. It was similar to the first but was faster and higher pitched. The rats responded to the change in the tune and began to turn away from the stranger and to begin to run up the Yar bridge. The stranger heard various gasps from the crowd that had now surrounded him.

The rats bounded up the bridge to its highest point, and then the most terrifying thing happened! The rats leaped clean over the stone wall to one side of the bridge and fell headfirst into the river. Thousands upon thousands of rats each followed the song of the pipe and jumped to their deaths. Shrieking came from several women in the crowd and some even cheered, but most were completely awestruck by the sight.

As the stranger watched the rats falling to their deaths, and watched the strong currents of the river wash them away, he cried. Tears were streaming down his cheeks, but he ensured that no one saw his face.

I wish that they didn't have to die! thought the stranger to himself.

The death of so many innocent animals to save a town of wicked people completely disgusted him.

I'd rather these wretched men and women drown than my babies!

Something then caught the stranger's eye that gave him some comfort. A rat had survived! He could see it climbing out of the water on the far bank. It quickly ran off toward a cluster of trees further up the riverbank. The stranger smiled to himself pleased.

I hope my baby goes on to live a full life and have pups! he thought.

The last of the rats jumped from the bridge and were then quickly taken by the river. The townsfolk cheered and clapped. The stranger then turned toward them all and gave a greatly exaggerated bow. The stranger was then swarmed by the townsfolk who picked him up and carried him on their shoulders like a hero from some long-forgotten tale. The stranger smiled and laughed but these expressions were a mere mask for the real pain he was feeling. The stranger allowed the people to carry him off toward town.

Every town reacts in the same way, he thought to himself. *They won't however, be as happy come tomorrow when I return for payment!*

CHAPTER 6

THOMAS & OWEN

The day that the rats plunged to their deaths in the river Yar was a day of great joy for the folk of Brading. On that day the news was carried out to the neighbouring towns and villages on the Wyght Island. All were told of the events that had happened and an invitation was given to a great celebration, that was to be had the following day. It was to celebrate the liberation of the town from the plague of rats.

It was around 11 o'clock that very next morning, that Thomas stood alongside Molly to watch the wagons and carts roll into town. Some carts were laden with crates upon crates of fresh fruits, and some with freshly baked bread and pastries. Some carts were piled with kegs of ale and other beverages. Thomas even saw one cart that was filled to the brim with pies. Most of the wagons, however, were filled with people. Families and communities from the island came to the festivities to celebrate with the townsfolk of Brading.

'Have you seen them yet?' asked Thomas optimistically.

'No,' said Molly.

'Where are they? Surely auntie must have heard the news and is bringing John back! They must be here by now! They couldn't have gone too far!'

'Maybe they'll be coming from the South entrance into town.

'Yes, maybe,' replied Thomas. 'There's no sign of them here, so let's head there.'

The two walked together through town and saw that the party was already well underway. There was music playing at various places along the street. Some were fiddlers and others were pipers, and there were even some with lutes and drums. Many people throughout the town were dancing and singing. Others were eating and drinking, and children were running and playing. There were also many men that were drunk already and some were even vomiting in the street. It truly was a party unlike any that Thomas had ever seen before.

'This is the biggest party I've ever seen!' said Molly in awe. 'It's wonderful that the rats are gone, but how about all those that we have lost! Surely we should be mourning their deaths first!'

'I know, It's disgraceful!' replied Thomas.

As they continued on they saw the Reverend Nicholas sitting in a high-backed leather chair, opposite the tavern, that was straining under his weight. He had a goblet in one hand and a leg of lamb in the other. He was laughing at some joke a nearby man was telling him. Food and spittle flew from his mouth as he laughed loudly.

Thomas then heard the priest talking about the stranger to the same man.

'That man with his pipe, is devious he is!' said the Reverend. 'Bringing those rats into our town and blackmailing us before getting rid of them!'

'I thought that Owen chap brought the rats?' said the man.

'I think they're probably in on it together! They'll get what's coming to them though! You mark my words, this time next week that stranger and Mr Smith will both be hanging in the main square with the crows for company!'

Thomas became angry and moved to respond but was quickly pulled away by Molly into a nearby alley.

'Don't get drawn into it with him!' she said. 'He's not worth the bother!'

'I know, but it's just so unfair!' he replied frustrated.

Molly hugged him close.

'We'll be ok my love. Soon we'll be able to leave this dreadful place!'

Thomas kissed her head.

'I can't wait!' he replied.

The two left the alley and continued South toward the other entrance to town. Both Thomas and Molly looked about to see if they could see aunt Emmy and John, but there was still no sign of either of them. As they walked, the crowds were getting larger and the roads more packed. The reason was becoming clear.

The crowds were gathered around a cart that was moving very slowly through town being pulled by a great horse. On top of the cart sat the stranger in a high-backed ornate chair. The stranger was wearing his same colourful outfit again and was playing a tune on his pipe that had all the people around dancing.

As Thomas walked, the Piper caught his eye and gave him a nod of acknowledgment while playing his merry tune. Thomas was still unsure of the Piper. He seemed nice enough, but there was something strange about him too. The Piper also looked familiar but Thomas could not work out where from. Thomas wondered if it was simply someone from one of the old towns they had lived in, or maybe it was a relative or someone his parents knew. He wasn't sure but kept thinking about it as they walked.

Thomas and Molly arrived at the South entrance to town. The merriments there were just as intense as the rest of the town they passed through. They asked others if they had seen Thomas' brother or aunt, but no one had. They searched around the crowds but there was still no sign of aunt Emmy or John. Thomas was beginning to become more and more worried about them, especially his brother. They waited an hour more before finally giving up.

Thomas slumped onto a nearby grassy knoll and cried into Molly's bosom. She hugged him and tried to reassure him and soothe him as best she could.

'I need to see Pa!' said Thomas after a while.

'The Mayor won't let you remember!' replied Molly.

'I know, and that's why I'm going to ask the Captain instead.'

'Good idea,' replied Molly. 'Come, let's go now before it gets too late.'

She pulled Thomas to his feet and the two walked back into town, hand in hand.

***

Owen was back at the lockup and in the stocks, but this time it was his feet the stocks held. He had been informed that the plague of rats had now gone and that the town was in celebration. Owen hoped that this might better improve his chances of freedom, but doubted it. The sound of keys and the unlocking of the lockup door caused Owen to turn to see who was entering. He had been expecting one of the guards with his ration of bread and water for the day but was shocked to see Thomas in the doorway instead.

'You have five minutes!' said the guard who had opened the door. Thomas stepped into the lockup and the guard shut the door behind him.

'Pa? What have they done to you?' said Thomas who quickly dashed over to him to hug him.

Owen considered himself a strong man, not necessarily physically but definitely emotionally, but the sight of Thomas and his warm embrace caused Owen to burst into tears. Thomas held his head and comforted him.

'Oh Thomas! My good sweet boy Thomas! I promise you that I never did any of the things that those men said I did!' said Owen through sobs and tears.

'I know, Pa,' said Thomas consolingly.

'I would never hurt a hair on your Ma's head. She's my sweetheart and she always will be!'

'Pa! You must listen because time is short!'

'I'm sorry my boy. Speak,'

Owen composed himself as Thomas spoke.

'The rats have desecrated this town, and many lives and livelihoods have been lost. The rats are now gone, but they are determined to lay the blame on you!'

'I promise you, my son, this is all lies!'

'I know Pa,' replied Thomas lowering his voice. 'And that's why we need to get you out of here!'

'It's no good. There's nothing we can do but hope justice prevails.'

'No Pa, we can't rely on hopes or miracles. We need to act! Listen, I'm going to arrange an escape.'

'No Son, you listen! I want you to take care of your brother and sister.'

'But Pa, there's a chance we can get you out!'

'No Thomas!' replied Owen. 'I will not have you risking yourself for me. I need you to step up and be a man. Take care of Lucy and John! Tell them that I love them very much.'

Thomas opened his mouth to tell his Father that John was probably dead but then closed it again. His Father had been through so much and the news might finish him off, so Thomas kept quiet.

The keys in the door began to rattle and the door opened.

'I love you Pa, we all do,' said Thomas fighting back the tears.

'I love you too son and I am so very proud of you.' replied Owen who started to cry again.

Thomas left the room and looked back to see his Father with his head hung low, quietly sobbing to himself.

CHAPTER 7

THE CAPTAIN & LUCY

Captain Campion wandered slowly around the village green taking in the various sights that could be seen. He had not long ago given permission for Thomas Smith to visit his father in the lockup. The Captain supposed that the boy was there now.

Around the edge of the green were stalls of various types. Some were selling food or drink, some were selling clothes and tools, and some had games that could be played. The Captain's gaze, however, was drawn to a stage that had been set up in the centre of the green around the town maypole. On the stage was the Mayor about to give a speech to the large crowd that had gathered around him.

'Ladies and Gentlemen,' the Mayor began. 'We stand on the precipice of greatness! Yesterday, this town had been plagued by the vilest of God's creations but, despite their evil intent, God has delivered us! He sent a saviour, just as he had sent one to Daniel in the lion's pit, and just as he sent one to Lot in the city of Sodom!'

The crowd gave a cheer and clapped. The Captain watched the Mayor in fascination. He was certainly a good public speaker. The crowd was hanging off his every word.

'I'm here to tell you today that the town of Brading will never fall! In every test that we have faced, we have triumphed! The French, the plague, the rats, all have tried to destroy our town but they have all failed!'

The crowd gave another loud cheer.

'We will stand forever!'

The crowd clapped and cheered and shouted "forever!' in unison.

The Mayor then introduced Lady Barton to the platform. She was another individual that the town loved. Lady Barton spoke of the great generosity of the townsfolk and why they should continue to be even more charitable now.

The Captain began to slowly walk around the edge of the green and stopped now and then to browse a stall or two.

As he was walking he spotted Carruthers talking to a lady of class who was evidently not interested in talking to him. The Captain watched with a smirk on his face looking at the pathetic attempt of his counterpart to flirt with the lady. It eventually led to the lady slapping Carruthers clean across the face and walking off. The Captain laughed to himself and walked over to the Sargent who was now rubbing his sore cheek.

'I see your luck with the ladies hasn't improved!' he said smiling.

'You can't win them all Captain,' he replied. 'Besides, I think she secretly liked me.'

'Even though she slapped you?'

'I was probably just coming over too strong. I'll try again with her later.'

'Poor you Carruthers,' jested the Captain. 'You're just too young to understand the ways of a woman!'

'I'm thirty-four Captain!' replied Carruthers acting offended.

'Exactly!' said the Captain still smiling. 'Come, let's take a walk and see what we can see.'

At that, the two men headed away from the village green and walked up the main street of the town.

***

It was late afternoon and the party was starting to get into full swing. Lucy sat leaning against a wall behind a group of children who were watching a puppet show. The show was re-enacting the story of the Piper and the rats, with a few little comedy moments thrown in to make the children laugh.

The Piper, earlier that day, had been paraded through the town where he had been treated like a hero. During the party the Piper danced with the women, drank with the men, and he entertained the children. The townsfolk loved him. Lucy though was suspicious of him and kept herself to herself. She leaned her head back against the wall and wondered where Thomas was. Lucy hadn't seen Thomas since that morning and presumed that he was still with the blonde-haired girl. Lucy had never seen Thomas in love and it scared her to see how much love can change a person. She had never really thought about love before. She had always assumed that it was something that happened to you when you were a lot older. She reminisced on the few boys that she had kissed when young, but those times were for fun or in response to a dare.

She then began to think about her younger brother John and whether he would eventually marry despite his being unable to walk. It was thinking of John that brought a tear to her eye.

Where are you John? she thought to herself.

Lucy began to get upset and so put her face in her hands and started to cry. As she sat there sobbing a man approached. The man was dressed in a long black coat. He lowered himself and sat down beside her. Lucy assumed it was one of the rat catchers she had been working with.

'Hi Mr Brady,' she said.

Lucy then looked across and noticed that it wasn't him.

'Oh, I'm sorry,' she stammered. 'I thought you were someone else.'

'That's ok little Miss,' the man replied. 'I saw you crying and thought that maybe you had lost your folks. Was going to see if you needed any help.'

'Thank you for your kindness. I'm not lost. I'll be ok. It's just been a terrible few days.'

'What's your name?' he asked.

'I'm Lucy.'

'It's good to meet you, Lucy. My name is Sir Timerus.'

'You're a sir! Were you knighted?'

'Of course! I still have the very blade that I was knighted with.'

'Wow! It's good to meet you, Sir.'

Lucy sat up and flattened out her dress and brushed off some dirt.

'Are you enjoying the party Lucy?' he asked.

'Not really, I'm a little worried about this Piper chap who killed the rats.'

'What do you mean? He did a good thing didn't he?'

'Yes, I suppose so,' she replied. 'But I've heard bad things about him. Do you think he's dangerous?'

Sir Timerus rubbed his chin with his hand and appeared to think deeply.

'That is a good question Lucy, and the answer is very simple. Yes! He is dangerous!'

'How do you know that?' she asked.

'Because Lucy, you should always view any stranger as dangerous.'

'Really?'

'Yes! Take me for example,' he said. 'You don't know me, you only know my name. To you, I'm a stranger and so you need to be wary. Now obviously I'm not dangerous, but you don't know that. Only by getting to know someone can you really trust them.'

What Sir Timerus had said made sense. Lucy had come to realise, since being in this town, that not everyone was as good, or as virtuous, as they would have you believe.

'I don't mean to frighten you, Lucy,' said Sir Timerus breaking the silence.

'You didn't frighten me, I was just thinking about what you said. So can I trust you?'

'Let's talk some more and maybe you can decide for yourself.'

Lucy agreed and the two sat and talked for a time. About an hour later Sir Timerus got up, bid Lucy farewell, and walked up the street.

CHAPTER 8

THE STRANGER & THOMAS

After his conversation with the girl named Lucy, the Piper headed toward the bull ring in the town square. The bull ring was where one of the main events of the year took place on the Wyght island and the Piper felt impelled to watch.

The Piper's understanding of the event was that one of the rich folk of Brading provided a well-nurtured bull that was attached to the famed bull ring in the middle of the town. The bull ring itself was literally just a hard metal ring sticking out of the ground. The attached bull was then set upon by the Mayor's dog who killed the beast in front of the crowd. After the killing, the crowd would then begin to carve meat from the dead beast that they could then take home to eat. This was a Brading town tradition that had gone on for over a century and was well known on the Wyght island.

As the Piper approached, he saw that a large crowd had already gathered around the bull ring. There were hundreds of people and they were working themselves up into a frenzy. Each of the individuals had a knife, or a blade in hand, ready for what was to come. The bull itself stood oblivious to what was about to happen.

The Piper found himself a good position in which to watch the event unfold. A few minutes later a bell began to ring from toward the Town Hall. It was a handbell that was being rung by one of the town guards who walked up the street leading a procession of people behind him.

As the group approached the bull ring, the bell ringing stopped and the crowd parted to allow the group through. Following the guard were the Mayor, Lord Mulberry, and one of the Mayor's slaves who handled a large dog on a leash. The Piper saw that the slave appeared to be of oriental descent. His eyes were slanted and he had a thin moustache that hung long on both sides of his mouth. The Piper also noticed that the dog was a bloodhound. It had obviously been bred to hunt and kill. The crowd kept their distance from the dog who had now begun growling and snarling at the chained-up bull. The bull moved uneasily away as best it could.

As soon as the Mayor entered the centre of the crowd he raised his arms which caused the crowd to clap and cheer. The Mayor bowed in response and then quieted the crowd with his hands.

'Today is a special day my friends,' Lord Mulberry began. 'This is that time of year when we give something back to the community! Each of you has worked hard to keep the Wyght Island thriving. And it is time to step up and take a small token of our esteem and thanks. Our gift to you is a piece of the best meat that can be found on the whole Island.'

The crowd cheered and clapped again.

'Release the hound,' shouted the Mayor.

At that, Lord Mulberry's slave untethered the dog from its leash and the dog immediately sprang into action.

The dog charged toward the bull with its teeth exposed and with fury in its eyes. The bull, however, saw it coming and tried to make its stand. As the dog leaped, the bull tried to hit it full-on with its horns. The chain however stifled it, causing it to miss. The dog attacked ferociously. The bull moaned in pain and tried to buck and kick the dog off of it. The dog let go and dove again for the bull tearing great chunks of flesh out of it. Within a few minutes, the bull was dead.

The crowd clapped and cheered, and after the dog was tethered again, the people lined up. Each person in turn then began to cut a piece of flesh from the dead beast with their knives and other sharp instruments. The Piper left the scene disgusted with the inhumane way the people acted. He was also disgusted with the mistreatment of such a fine beast. He left the bloodthirsty crowd to their bloody reward.

***

It was late in the evening when Thomas walked home with Lucy. He had spotted her sitting on the floor against a wall, opposite a puppet show. Her eyes had lit up when she had seen him approach. He had reached out his hand to her and she took it, and the two began to walk home together.

They passed ones that were tipsy and drunk and even saw a large number of townsfolk that had passed out on the floor. They passed groups that were dancing, and they also saw the bull ring which was still a bloody mess after the butchering of the bull.

The two had walked in silence waiting until they reached home. It was when they got home that Thomas aired his concerns to Lucy and his great plan.

'I don't think it's a good idea, Thomas,' said Lucy concerned. 'If anything were to go wrong it could land you in a lot of trouble, or even worse get you killed!'

'Honestly Lucy, I've sat down and worked it all out with Molly. Pa is due to go before the court in two days, and if he is found guilty he will be hung on Saturday. That gives us four days to get everything ready and to put all our plans into place.'

'Four days isn't long!'

'I know, and that's why we need to act as soon as possible!'

'I still don't get how we can do this!' said Lucy sceptically.

'I promise you we can because we will have a secret weapon,' replied Thomas confidently.

'What secret weapon?'

'A pistol!'

'A pistol? Where are you going to get a pistol?'

'We're going to steal it!'

'How are you going to steal it?'

'I'm not. You are!' said Thomas smiling.

Lucy sat back in her chair feeling confused.

'Tell me your great plan for stealing the pistol!' she said.

CHAPTER 9

OWEN & THE CAPTAIN

It was the morning after the town celebrations and all was quiet. The sun was shining through the bars of the lockup casting beams of light on Owen's face, which woke him from his sleep. Owen stirred and was feeling better for the first time in a long time. Ever since he had been imprisoned, his wounds and fever had been treated and now he finally felt on the road to recovery. The timing was perfect as Owen had an important decision to make. This decision was going to affect the rest of his life, and he now felt more mentally stable to decide.

Should I plead guilty or not guilty? he thought to himself.

Owen knew that if he pleaded not guilty, one of two things would happen. He would either be found innocent by the court and set free, or he would be found guilty and hung. He did not doubt that he would hang if he pleaded not guilty. The Mayor had it in for him and he was extremely influential. On the other hand, Owen had the option to plead guilty and go to the asylum. If he pleaded guilty to the charges against him, he would be sent to the nut house, which was a place worse than hell itself. The doctor that visited him made an offer that could see him free in about a year, but he would have to undergo experiments first.

It was the choice of life or death. Logically he should choose life, but at what cost would that come? He wasn't too sure of the answer. The time to make his decision was fast approaching.

***

Captain Campion entered the lockup and it stank of faeces, urine, and sweat. The Captain carried on without so much as a grimace, however, Sargent Carruthers was following and he was visibly unimpressed by the smell. The Captain saw that Owen was still secure by his legs in the stocks, but he appeared in better spirits than he had been of late. He didn't appear as miserable or downtrodden as he previously did when the Captain had seen him before.

'Good morning gentlemen,' said Owen. 'Or is it afternoon? It's difficult to tell without being able to see where the sun is sitting.'

'It's morning Mr Smith,' replied the Captain. 'How are you feeling?'

'I'm feeling better than I have been, but I still want to be out of this awful place!'

'We're glad you're feeling better. As you know, it's your court case tomorrow. One of the Sister's from Newport will be presiding over the proceedings. As we have previously explained to you if you plead not guilty but are found guilty you will hang for your crimes. If you however plead guilty now, we will arrange for you to serve your time at the asylum. You have previously stated that you are not guilty, but I need to inform you that the case against you is very strong indeed.'

'The evidence they have against me Captain is circumstantial. The Mayor simply has a vendetta against me.'

'That is all well and good Mr Smith but again, there is nothing to support your claims. We even looked into your claim that you returned to the Kyngs Arms that night in order to ascertain if you had an alibi, but no one could vouch for you. Also, the fact that the evidence is circumstantial is not enough for this case to be thrown out. As you know, the Wyght

Island operates its laws and judicial system in a very different way to the mainland.'

'I know Captain.' said Owen with his head down.

'If you plead guilty today, we will speak on your behalf so that you are treated well.'

Owen raised his head.

'Treated well? At the asylum? Is that even possible?'

'To be honest Mr Smith I have never been to the asylum, but I will do what I can.'

'How long can I have to think about it?' asked Owen.

'We'll give you until dusk and then we'll return for your answer.'

CHAPTER 10

LUCY & THE STRANGER

It was early morning when Lucy crept around the back of the building containing the town pistol. The building was a Folly Tower known as "Kyngs Folly" to the local folk. It was located on a hill in a woodland area, between the town and the Haven docks. As far as towers are concerned, this one was very small. Lucy was told that there were twelve Folly Towers on the Wyght Island and that each was owned by one of the ruling Brothers.

This tower itself was a simple structure. It was similar to a house in diameter but it had three levels. The lower level was for a guard who lived at the tower who would care for its maintenance and security. The guard would also attend to the Brother's needs if he ever visited. The next two levels were for the Brother. No one knew what it was like inside, but it was well known that the Brother's pistol was kept there.

It was taught on the island that when a man was appointed to the Brotherhood, he was always served with a pistol. The pistol, though live, was more symbolic and decorative than practical. It was a symbol of what the Brother was and what he stood for.

There were very few firearms on the island and Thomas had said that this would be the easiest one to get.

Lucy didn't understand why she was the one that had to steal the pistol until she saw the tower. The tower was a defensive structure but it had several arrow slits that looked like a child could squeeze through them. On closer inspection, she could see that she should be able to do it. The Brother wasn't there, hadn't been there in years apparently, but the guard would be. Lucy had to find a way to get in without alerting the guard.

Lucy crept around the back of the building, cursing Thomas mentally as she went. She had a bad feeling about this venture and wished he was there instead. Even if he was hiding nearby it would have given her some confidence, but he had other plans to put in place for the escape.

Lucy saw the guard's door and tiptoed closer to it. Fortunately, it was closed. Lucy needed to work out if the guard was inside or was patrolling somewhere outside. She hadn't seen the guard when she approached, but that didn't mean he wasn't out there. She crept up to the door and put her ear to it. Snoring could clearly be heard coming from inside.

Good, she thought to herself. *This is going to be a lot easier than I thought.*

She moved slowly around to the front of the tower. There were steps leading up to the main door, and above the door was a stone overhang designed to protect the door from rain.

Lucy began to climb the steps. As she reached the door she tried the handle hoping that fortune would favour her, unfortunately, it didn't. The door was locked tight.

Lucy climbed onto the stone balustrading that led up alongside the steps and reached for the stone overhang above the door. She stretched hard ensuring that she didn't fall and managed to gain a good grip. With her hands gripping the overhang, and with one foot against a jutting piece of stone sticking out the wall, she managed to hoist herself up.

She stood on the overhang and reached for the nearest arrow slit. The arrow slit was vertical but also had a horizontal slit through the middle. This middle part produced a larger gap which she believed would be big enough for her to squeeze through.

She reached up to the arrow slit and, with much tugging and twisting, she was able to pull herself through. After pulling herself through, however, she hit the wooden floor hard. This not only hurt her arm and shoulder but caused a loud bang. She held her breath and listened out for any sound that may come from the guard's room down below. She heard nothing but stayed still.

After a few minutes of silence, she climbed to her feet, brushed her skirt down, and looked around the room. The room was small with a desk against one wall and a staircase against another. On the wall above the desk were a map of the town of Brading and another map of the island. There were several books in a bookcase against the same wall, and various artifacts were scattered around the room on wooden shelves.

Lucy stepped toward the desk but froze. She heard a sound. The sound was the jingling of keys. She looked around quickly and there was nowhere to hide. She heard the key enter the lock, and so she quickly climbed up the staircase at the back of the room to the top floor.

Lucy was now in the Brother's sleeping chamber. A large four-poster bed was the main feature of the room. There was also a clothes closet and a glass cabinet in which she could see the Brother's pistol.

Lucy then heard footsteps on the floorboards in the room below. The footsteps were then heard climbing the staircase. Lucy dived under the bed and hoped that she wouldn't be seen. She saw the guard's boots. The guard moved around the room and then stopped in front of the bed. She then saw the guard begin to get to his knees.

No! Lucy thought. *I can't be caught!*

Fear gripped her as she saw one hand lean on the floor. His chin came slowly into view and then there was a crash. Something smashed onto the floor downstairs. The guard quickly stood up and dashed down the staircase. Lucy heard the guard talking to himself.

'I knew something had got in here!' he said. 'Flaming pesky bird! Get out! Out!'

Lucy heard some commotion, and then heard the door close and the keys lock it. Lucy got out from under the bed and moved toward one of the windows. She saw the guard descend the steps and head toward the back of the tower, presumably to his quarters. She breathed a sigh of relief and stood for a few moments composing herself. She then moved to the glass cabinet.

Inside the cabinet, she could see the Brother's famous pistol. The gold and silver of the pistol were beautiful and sparkling. She opened the cabinet and took the weapon out. It was heavy in her small hands and she handled it delicately. She then tucked the pistol into the back of her belt, which held up her skirt.

She was about to leave when she saw something odd. There was a pedestal against one of the walls. On the wall above was another map of the town of Brading, but it was the thing on the pedestal that drew Lucy's attention. It was a chessboard. This chessboard however was different from any others that she had seen. This chessboard was only half a board. On the board were the most beautiful of chess pieces she had ever seen, all lined up ready. These pieces looked as if they had been carved out of pure sapphire. She picked up one of the pawns and the weight of it shocked her. It was extremely heavy. She replaced the piece but noticed that some of the pieces were missing. A rook and bishop were missing, and also three pawns. She looked about but couldn't see them. It was strange seeing such a beautiful thing and wondered why half the board was missing and also some pieces. She knew she couldn't linger in the tower and so left the chessboard.

She descended the steps to the lower level, being careful not to make any noise.

Thomas will be so happy! she thought. *I can't wait to see his face!*

She was now on the lower level and was about to begin climbing out the arrow slit when the door swung open. Lucy jumped in shock, but instead of the guard standing there, it was Sir Timerus, the man that she had met at the town festival. He had the guard's keys in his hand.

'Come on little Miss,' he said. 'We better get you out of here!'

***

The Piper looked down at Lucy as the two headed back toward Brading. The tower was some way behind them, and the smoke rising from the chimneys in the town were becoming more visible.

'So what was all that about, young Lucy?' he asked.

Lucy pulled the pistol out from behind her back.

'I had to get this,' she said examining it closely.

'You need to be careful with that! It is a dangerous weapon! Why do you even want it?'

'I can't tell you, Sir.'

'You're planning to break your Pa out of the lockup!'

It wasn't a question.

'How do you know that?' asked Lucy.

The Piper waved a hand dismissing her question.

'Please be careful Lucy,' he said. 'That weapon is one of the fabled twelve. A weapon like that in the wrong hands is likely to explode! Take a look at my ear.'

The Piper took off his hat and Lucy stepped back seeing the remains of the right side of his head. His ear was missing and there were scars and burnt flesh surrounding the area where the ear had been. Lucy looked terrified and so the Piper put his hat back on.

'Don't worry girl,' he said putting a hand on her shoulder. 'Just be careful with that flintlock!'

'Flintlock?'

'Yes, that's the type of pistol it is.'

They both continued to walk and Lucy looked down at the flintlock in her hands. It was beautifully made and had wooden grips, and on the grips were carvings. The carvings were hard to make out. The Piper looked at Lucy examining the flintlock.

'Can you see what animal is carved there?' he said.

'No, I can't quite make it out.'

He took the weapon from her and knelt to show her the outline of the beast.

'Is it a bull, or maybe possibly a cow?' she replied still looking at it intently.

'It's a bull. It's the pistol of the Bull.'

He handed the weapon back and the two continued walking.

'Do you think you could help to free my Pa, Mr Timerus sir?'

'I'm afraid there would be little point Lucy!'

He stopped and turned toward her.

'Your Pa has already gone!'

'What? That can't be! Thomas said that we still had time!' she cried.

'No, your Pa is now in the asylum, but don't worry Lucy, your Pa will be fine and you may even see him again.'

Tears began to slowly run down Lucy's face. The stranger wanted to comfort her but knew he couldn't. Lucy looked again at the flintlock and reached it out toward him.

'You had better take this. We won't be needing it anymore.' she said.

The Piper gently pushed the pistol away, back toward Lucy.

'No Lucy, that weapon still has a role to play in this story. Now you must listen! You must ensure that you give it to the girl called Molly!'

'Molly? But why?'

'That I cannot say, but it must go into her hands.'

Lucy nodded confused and tucked the flintlock back into her belt.

The two began to walk again and the town was getting closer.

'I need to tell you something little Miss, but maybe you already know.'

'What's that?'

'I'm the Piper!'

Lucy's heart began to beat fast but she kept herself composed and carried on walking.

'No, I didn't know.' she replied.

The two continued on for a few minutes in silence, but then Lucy spoke.

'Can I ask you a question, Sir?'

'Of course!'

'Did you really steal children from a town many years ago?'

'Where did you hear that?'

'One of the rat catchers told me,' she replied.

'In answer to your question, no, I did not.'

'I'm relieved,' she said smiling.

'I didn't take any children Lucy, but I once knew a man who did. And I intend to do the same here!'

'What?' she replied suddenly frightened.

'I am going to save the children from this terrible place!'

Lucy wanted to get away from him, but he grabbed her shoulder.

'Listen to me, Lucy. I need to tell you something that will save you and the other children of this town, including your brother!'

'Thomas can look after himself!' she replied sharply.

'I'm not talking about Thomas. I mean John. Your brother John is alive!'

'Alive! Where is he?'

'He is safe and he is waiting for you and his friends. Let me tell you more, but you must only tell Thomas what I allow you to tell him because John's life depends upon it.'

'Yes Sir,' said Lucy.

The two continued walking and the Piper told her everything. Almost everything.

CHAPTER 11

THOMAS & MOLLY

Thomas sat in a chair in the cottage that they had first moved into when arriving in the town of Brading. Considering the damage that had been done to the other properties in town, the cottage looked good. There were a few places where it appeared that the rats had got in, and there was also an annoying clicking sound that came and went sporadically. Other than that, Bugle Cottage was in very good shape, Thomas however, was not. He sat with his head in his hands, massaging his forehead. He had his eyes closed as if in deep thought, and his right leg was twitching up and down in frustration.

'How can this be?' he said out loud to no one in particular, even though Lucy and Molly were with him. 'Did he say when this happened? When they took Pa?'

'Last night apparently,' Lucy replied.

'What did you see when you went there, Molly?'

'The lockup was empty and there were no guards anywhere. What Lucy said seems to be right.'

'Did he say anything else, Lucy?' Thomas asked.

'Two things. Firstly, he said that Pa would be ok and that we would see him again.'

'How does he know that?' said Molly. 'Is the man some kind of prophet!'

'I don't know about that, but everything he has said has always happened,' said Thomas. 'What was the other thing he said?'

'The second thing he said was that we will still need the pistol and that Molly must have it. She must keep it with her at all times.'

Thomas picked up the pistol from the small table next to him. He felt the weight of it in his hands. It was a beautiful piece and obviously quite old. He rubbed his thumb over the engraving of the bull. He then passed the pistol to Molly.

'I don't want it!' she said refusing to take it.

'I know, but if the Piper said you must have it, then there must be a good reason. Maybe it'll play a part in us seeing Pa again.'

Molly took the pistol into her now-shaking hands.

'I'm not sure about this,' she said.

'Just keep it with you. Keep it secret, keep it safe.' Thomas replied.

Molly lifted her foot onto a stool, pulled the skirt of her dress up, and tucked the pistol into her thigh-length stocking. She then straightened her dress out again.

'So what do we do now?' said Molly.

'We're going to get out of here, that's what!' replied Thomas. 'Let's get off this island and the three of us head North to start a new life!'

'Do you think we can do it?' asked Molly.

'Definitely my love,' he replied.

Thomas stood and gave Molly a hug.

'I want to be with you forever,' he said.

'And I want nothing more than to be with you!' Molly replied.

Thomas noticed that Lucy sat motionless and appeared to be in a daze.

'She must be missing Pa,' thought Thomas.

He was wrong.

***

Molly was eager to leave town. After talking with Thomas and Lucy, she had gone back to her barn where she packed a few of her belongings into a large wicker basket.

She wanted to say goodbye to her father and so walked up to the main house. Her stepmother answered the door and told her that he was not home and that Molly should get away from the house. Molly thought that her Father must be at the Kyngs Arms and so decided to head there to see him one final time. It was on this short journey that Molly learned some interesting information.

As Molly headed down the Main Street toward the tavern she heard a group of men coming up quickly behind her, talking amongst themselves. She moved out of their way to allow them to pass but caught a few words of their conversation.

'Who cares what he says or does! He's just a stranger, and it was probably him that brought the rats here in the first place!'

Molly noticed that it was the priest who was speaking. She couldn't mistake his booming voice or his girth as he strode past with the other men.

'I agree,' said one of the other men whom Molly couldn't identify. 'Why should we pay money to someone such as him!'

The discussion faded as the men walked further away from Molly.

I can't believe what they're saying about him, thought Molly. *After all he's done for the town!*

After a few minutes, Molly arrived at the Kyngs Arms and walked in. The tavern was quiet but Molly knew that soon the tavern would be packed with patrons. She looked and saw her father slouched at the bar. He was asleep. The side of his face was on the counter in a puddle of ale. Molly quickly moved over to him and tried to wake him.

'Wake up father,' she said shaking him. 'I have something important I need to tell you!'

Her father's head rolled about as she gripped his shoulders.

'Father! Please wake up!'

'That'll do no good honey!' said Mr Cooper from further up the bar. 'He'll be completely out of it for a few hours. I'll send him home when he's awake and sobered up a bit.'

Molly welled up. She had hoped that she would be able to say goodbye properly. She took off her shawl which had been around her neck, folded it up neatly, and put it on the counter. She then laid her father's head on the shawl which acted as a cushion. She then kissed her father's forehead and walked back out the tavern. The tears were streaming down her face as she left and she began to sob as she walked back up the road.

Molly's crying was suddenly disturbed by shouting. Molly ducked into a nearby alley, wiping the tears from her face with her sleeve. She then peered out to see what the commotion was. She saw the five town council members, with several town guards, all shouting at the Piper.

'Get out of town!' shouted the Mayor.

'You're the antichrist!' shouted the reverend.

The five council members then began to pick up and throw at the Piper whatever was close to hand, whether it be rotten food or stones. The Piper strode out of the town without even looking back.

What has happened to this town? she thought to herself. *I knew it was bad but this is terrible! I can't wait to leave this dreadful place!*

After the shouting had stopped, and the council members had walked away laughing, Molly headed back to meet Thomas at the smithy. He was there preparing the donkey and cart for their long journey ahead.

CHAPTER 12

THE CAPTAIN & LUCY

Sargent Carruthers poured the Captain a shot of whisky as the two sat at a table in the Kyngs Arms. It was their last night in Brading before heading back to London. The case they had been sent to investigate was now closed. Mary Smith had been laid to rest and her husband and murderer, Owen Smith, was currently en route to the Wyght Asylum. The problem with the vermin had also been resolved too. The Piper had successfully rid the town of the rats, so much so, that no rat had been seen since.

The Captain downed his shot of whiskey without so much as a slight grimace. Sargent Carruthers on the other hand drank his whisky slowly, and every sip pulled his lips back over his teeth.

'It'll be good to get home, don't you agree Captain.' said Carruthers.

'Yes, it'll be nice to be back under my own roof and sleeping in my own bed. I've even missed London!'

'I know what you mean Captain. I miss the hustle and bustle of the old place. I miss the ladies too!' said Carruthers with a smile on his face.

'Oh Carruthers, you're so eager to go and sow your wild oats!' said the Captain smiling.

'Of course. I have a lot of sowing to catch up on since we've been away if you know what I mean.'

'Unfortunately, I do!' said the Captain raising an eyebrow.

'Can I ask you a question Captain?'

'Of Course.'

'A few days ago during the town meeting, you said that the Wyght Asylum was one of the toughest prisons in the world and that only the islanders and top officials know about the place.'

'Yes, I remember,' said the Captain as he poured another shot of whiskey.

'Well, I asked how that information had never left the island and spread around, and you said that it was a good question for another time. Well, this is another time. Spill the beans.'

'Ok Carruthers, but I'm trusting you more than I trust most. You must take this information to the grave!'

'Of course Captain, I swear!'

'The Wyght Island itself is a prison!'

'A prison?'

'Yes, you see, hundreds of years ago the Wyght Island served as a penal colony. All criminals, whether male or female, were exiled from England to the island. The original plan was for the criminals to just fend for themselves on the island, or to die trying. It was even thought that the criminals may even end up killing each other, but that didn't happen. The criminals began to build communities, marry, and have children. They attempted to lead a normal life, and even formed their own laws and a type of government.'

'Wow!' said Carruthers.

'No one on the mainland had any idea what was happening until the fateful day that an imperial ship was shipwrecked on the island. The soldiers on that vessel expected hostility from the islanders, due to their past criminal nature, but instead were given help. The ship was repaired and the islanders helped the soldiers to return home.'

The Captain took a mouthful of whisky, while Carruthers sat engrossed in the tale.

'After the soldiers returned they reported what they found, but the King was not happy. He thereby put security measures in place so that no one could ever leave the island. There are military ships that patrol the waters surrounding the island, and there's even a great watchtower in Portsmouth where guards watch the island through telescopes.'

'How about the merchants that sail and dock here? Surely they know the real story of the island?'

'To them, it's a normal place, but every ship that leaves the island is boarded and searched by imperial ships. Anyone without a signed formal document is hung. Even the Captain of the ship itself would face severe punishment, possibly imprisonment or even hanging, and so they refuse to take anyone that doesn't have a formal document.'

'I'm shocked Captain!' said Carruthers stunned. 'How do the islanders feel about it?'

'Most don't know. They're happy with their lives here. They believe the island is just a normal place.'

'What happens though, when new criminals come here?'

'Very few come here now except for those most dangerous. They're immediately taken to the asylum in the middle of the island, where they're normally never heard from again.'

'That is quite a tale!'

The two sat in silence for a few moments.

'I'm looking forward to leaving tomorrow, and even more so now!' said the Sargent. 'I don't want to stay in this cesspit any longer than I need to!'

'I'll drink to that!' Replied the Captain.

The two men clinked their glasses and downed the last of their drinks. The Sargent began coughing as the whiskey went down.

'Let's get packed, ready for the off tomorrow,' said the Captain.

The two men stood to leave when the door to the tavern burst open. All in the tavern looked toward the door startled.

A man stood in the doorway panting and covered in soot.

'Quick, we need help! The school is on fire!'

***

Lucy sat on the doorstep with a basket on her lap. The basket contained a few of her personal things, and a few mementos to remind her of Ma, Pa, and John. Thomas and Molly were at the smithy preparing for the journey. They had said that they would be along to pick her up before they left. And so Lucy waited, eager to be off.

The tears ran gently down her face as she reflected on how much things had changed since she and her family had arrived in Brading. She genuinely thought that this would finally be the place where her family could settle down and be happy.

It was those disgusting rats who were to blame, but it was the Piper who had saved them all. She liked the Piper but was still wary of him. Clint said that the Piper was a known criminal that blackmailed towns and stole children, but after her discussion with the Piper, she was beginning to like and admire him. The Piper had said to her to not trust anyone until she got to know them, and she had got to know him.

Ever since his arrival, he had helped everyone, but it had been everyone else that had turned on him. She had heard a lot of negative talk about him at the town party, and it was Clint and his two associates who were apparently hunting him. The same men she noted who had been pretty deceitful themselves.

She really wanted to leave the island with Thomas and Molly and longed to start a new life where the pain of this place could be left behind, but what if what the Piper had told her was true? The Piper had told her that soon he would come and gather all the children. He said that if she wanted to see John again, then she would need to follow him too. Follow him to his cave of wonders. She desperately wanted to tell Thomas everything the Piper had said, but the Piper had warned her that it could cost John his life if she did.

She didn't know what to do but sat thinking about it. After much thought, she decided that she would tell Thomas. The burden of deciding what to do about it was too heavy for her to bear alone. As soon as he and Molly returned, she would tell them everything.

Thomas will know what to do, she thought to herself. *If only they would hurry up!*

It was while thinking of the whole situation that Lucy heard the music. Lucy stood, dropping her basket, mesmerised by the tune. The tune was from a pipe and that meant only one thing, the Piper was back. Lucy didn't want to see the Piper. She wanted to see Thomas and tell him everything she knew, but the song impelled her to move. She felt herself losing control and felt her willpower drifting away. She immediately began to run toward the sound of the music. She was suddenly desperate to see the Piper again and to see the fabled cave of wonders.

CHAPTER 13

THE STRANGER & THOMAS

The Piper leaned with his back against the crossroads sign in the town square as he played his pipe. The smoke that rose from the burning school filled his nostrils. A large number of townsfolk had run past him to help put out the flames at the Northern end of town. They didn't give him a second glance. It was when the streets were bare again that the children began to arrive.

The first of the children to arrive had big smiles on their faces and were happy to see the Piper. Within a few minutes, there was a small crowd. The children of the town that were gathered were all no older than twelve, except for the girl Lucy who was a little older. The Piper had seen her arrive and gave her a wink. The Piper then began to sing and dance and head away from the centre of town. The thirty or so children followed, skipping and clapping, full of happiness. The girl Lucy followed behind caught in the same mood as the other children. The Piper sang about a cave of wonders where the children would live happily ever after:

Follow me, my little friends, for wonders you're about to see,
a place of joy, a place of fun, a place that's ruled by me.
You'll never grow old, and never die young, and never be sick again,
you'll never cry, or ever mourn, or ever feel hurt or pain.
New fathers and mothers you will receive, who'll show you perfect love,
they'll hug and feed and cherish you, just like our God above.

You'll run and dance and play about, in the meadows, and in the trees,
where all the animals live in peace, even the lions, the tigers and bees.
So come and follow me my friends, and put away those frowns,
my cave of wonders lie up there, high upon the Downs.

The children loved the words he sang and were drawn by what he said. The children happily followed the Piper as he headed out of town, and toward the great hills of the Brading Downs.

***

Thomas and Molly had met at the smithy where he had prepared the donkey and cart for the journey ahead. They had a good supply of food, including salted meats and fish. There was also an adequate supply of fresh water, in large clay pots with lids. Thomas had also packed large sheets of fabric along with poles, ropes, and pegs, in order to create a tent if needed. Everything was ready. All that they needed to do now was to pick up Lucy, and the last of their things, from the old cottage.

On route from the smithy to the cottage, Molly told Thomas what had happened with her stepmother and father. Thomas felt her pain and sympathised as best he could, holding her hand as he held the reigns of the donkey. Molly then told of the events of what unfolded with the Piper and the Town council members. Thomas should have been shocked, but he wasn't.

As the two arrived they saw that Lucy wasn't waiting for them like arranged, but rather her personal belongings and her basket were strewn about all over the floor. Thomas and Molly checked the cottage but nobody was there. While searching the cottage, Thomas heard the strange clicking noise that he had heard before but now it had become a continuous grinding noise. It sounded like a mill stone turning, but a lot quieter and higher pitched. He followed the sound hoping it was Lucy. Thomas discovered that the sound was coming from the stable that was adjoined to the cottage.

'Molly!' called Thomas. 'Come to the stable, quick!'

Molly came running from the cottage.

'What's that noise?' she asked.

'I don't know.'

Thomas began to creep into the stable followed closely by Molly. There was a large spade close by that Thomas picked up ready. As the two approached the rear of the stable they saw movement in a small pile of hay.

'Do you think it's a rat?' asked Molly.

'Only one way to find out!' he replied.

At that, Thomas swung down the spade on the thing in the hay. There came a clank, the sound of metal hitting metal, and then the grinding noise stopped. Thomas used the spade to pull out whatever had been there. As he dragged it out, both he and Molly stepped back in fear. They saw that it was a Hamelin rat, but the creature wasn't moving. Thomas moved closer and bent to take a look at the rat.

'Be careful,' said Molly.

Thomas looked closely at the rat and noticed that it looked odd. It wasn't a rat! It was fake! Thomas picked it up and it was heavy. He could see inside the fake rat from where the spade had damaged it. It had a metal frame inside with several cogs in place. The eyes were both small white pebbles and the fur was like goats hair, but even more coarse. Thomas showed it to Molly.

'What is that thing?' she asked.

'It looks like the so called Hamelin rat! It's a fake! Its just some sort of contraption covered in goats hairs!'

Thomas tossed it to the ground where it clanked onto the wooden floor.

'We need to find Lucy and get out of here. Something bad is going to happen. The town has been fooled by the Piper and who knows what he's got in store!' he said.

'Let's find her!' Molly replied.

They both stepped out of the stable and began to shout her name in the street outside, but there was no response. The only clue they had of her whereabouts

was her footprints on the muddy ground. The two left the donkey and cart and eagerly followed her trail hoping she hadn't gone far.

The trail led to the centre of town and then they saw something strange. There wasn't just one set of footprints but rather there were dozens, and they were all small in size. They were the footprints of children. Thomas looked closely and saw one set of footprints that were different from all the others. They were big, a man's size footprint.

Thomas began to panic.

'Molly, you need to run and get help! The children are gone and it must be the Piper who took them!'

'What are you going to do?'

'Chase after them!'

At that, Thomas kissed her cheek and quickly ran in the same direction that the footprints were going.

CHAPTER 14

MOLLY & THE CAPTAIN

Molly ran as fast as she could toward the nearest guard tower. The discovery made by Thomas was chilling and it frightened her. The school in the town was ablaze, and now the children were all gone. Molly had to alert the town and the best way she knew how was to tell one of the guards at one of the watchtowers so they could sound the alarm. There were several watchtowers located around the edge of town and so Molly headed to the nearest one which was only a few minutes away. She hoped that help wouldn't come too late.

Molly arrived at the tower but couldn't see the guard. She assumed the guard had left to help fight the fire. She opened the door to the tower and ascended the ladder which was made more difficult by her long dress. She clambered to the top, sweating and panting. As she reached the main platform, she could see the guard slumped in a corner.

He's asleep! She thought. *Unbelievable!*

She reached over to wake him. As she touched him, his body slumped to the floor. A knife was protruding from his chest and blood covered the front of his jerkin.

Molly backed away and screamed in fright. She was frightened and began to panic.

Get up, Molly! She thought. *Get up and ring the bell! Thomas needs help!*

Molly stood, still shaking, and reached for the rope to ring the bell.

Without any hesitation, she pulled on the rope as hard as she could. The bell rang loud and clear in the dark night sky. Molly pulled on the rope and rang the bell again, and again. In fact, Molly planned not to stop ringing it, until help came.

***

The fire at the school was still raging when the Captain heard the bell. It wasn't just the Captain that heard the bell, all the townsfolk heard it too. The Captain ran over to the Mayor who appeared to be temporarily frozen after hearing the ringing of the watchtower bell.

'My Lord, I will take ten men on horseback to deal with whatever the alarm may be. You continue to work with the folk to put out the fire and to stop it spreading!'

Lord Mulberry remained silent and dumbstruck causing the Captain to grab his shoulders.

'My Lord!'

'Sorry Captain,' replied the Mayor. 'Yes, carry on and I'll take charge here!'

Lord Mulberry continued to help fight the fire with the other townsfolk. He shouted orders for more water to be brought. The Captain ran over to Sargent Carruthers who was also helping to fight the fire.

'Sargent! Gather ten men with horses and meet me at the stable in five minutes!'

'Yes Captain,' replied Carruthers

The Sargent immediately set off to find some men who could help.

Captain Campion ran straight to the Kyngs Arms and charged through the doors. The tavern was empty with everything as it was before the fire began. The Captain ran up the stairs and entered his room. He quickly put on his hat and coat and unlocked his cupboard.

Inside was a rifle. He loaded it with ammunition, grabbed an additional pistol, and headed back out the room.

Five minutes later, Captain Campion arrived at the stable to find Sargent Carruthers with ten men all mounted on horses. The Captain tossed Carruthers the pistol. Carruthers caught it, checked the barrel, and holstered it toward the front of his body in his belt. The Captain mounted his own horse.

'Follow me men!' shouted the Captain.

The group left the stable and began to gallop out toward the sound of the bell which was still ringing.

The bell at the watchtower was used to warn the folk of Brading. Whether it was to warn of an impending attack, or the sighting of a criminal, or simply a woodland fire, the sound of the bell always gave the folk a terrible sense of foreboding.

When the Captain and his posse arrived they were expecting a similar reason for the alarm. They didn't however, expect to see a young lady, ringing the bell. The girl was shaking and crying, and ringing the bell in panic. There was no evidence of any impending danger from anywhere. The men reigned in at the bottom of the watchtower and the Captain called out to the young lady.

'Who are you? And why are you sounding the alarm?'

My name is Molly. I'm a local farmer's daughter! You must hurry! He's taken the children!'

'What children? And who has taken them?' replied the Captain.

'The children of the town! They're all gone! The Piper has led them away during the fire!'

'Are you sure of this?' asked the Captain.

'Yes, hurry!' said Molly now near hysteria.

'Where has he taken them?'

'I don't know!' replied Molly crying.

At that moment, they heard a man shouting and running toward them from the direction of the town. The man sounded young but they couldn't clearly identify him.

'Quick help! The children are gone! He's taken them! They're heading South!'

'Are you sure?' shouted the Captain.

'Yes! Quick! Hurry!'

The Captain turned to Carruthers.

'Sargent, you take five men and head South out of town. Try to pick up the trail. I'll take the other men and try to cut them off!'

'Yes sir!' replied Carruthers.

At that, he motioned for the five closest men to follow him and the small group headed South back into the main part of town.

The Captain, with the five remaining men, headed South-West.

CHAPTER 15

LUCY & THE STRANGER

The Piper led the children skipping and dancing to the entrance of a large cave on the Brading Downs, above the town. As the children approached, Lucy recognised a man sitting on a horse with a wagon. It was Clint. He smiled at the children with menacing eyes.

'You got them all then?' said Clint.

'Of course,' replied the Piper. 'Any trouble?'

'No, the plan has worked beautifully. Hopper did a good job sending them in the wrong direction. That boy is a great runner, so he should be here any moment. Shall we start loading the children onto the wagon?'

Lucy's heart dropped. She didn't understand what was going on. Was John alive? Was there a cave of wonders? She was confused. She noticed that the other children looked confused too. Their smiles were now fading and fear began to be seen in their eyes. They were beginning to look visibly scared and shaken.

Clint saw the look of confusion in Lucy's eyes, so began to laugh and mock her.

'Little Miss Lucy! It's good to see you. I did warn you not to trust him!'

Clint continue to laugh, but at that moment, Hopper appeared from around a corner.

'Good work Lad,' said Clint smiling.

'Everything go as planned?' asked the Piper.

Hopper gave a thumbs up while trying to catch his breath.

'Good. Good,' said the Piper.

The Piper reached into his coat and pulled out a pistol. He then shot Clint in the forehead. Clint's horse neighed in fright and then bucked Clint's dead body to the ground. As the horse fled it caused the wagon to topple over. Blood began to pool around the dead man's head and his body began to twitch. Lucy and the other children screamed and backed further into the cave. The Piper then aimed at Hopper who raised his hands. Lucy was terrified and completely confused about what was happening.

'What's going on Brady? Why did you kill old Clint?' said Hopper.

'Because he was a foul pervert who was happy to sell children as slaves. He was a despicable man!'

'That was the plan though. That's what we all agreed, including you!'

'Oh yes I played along, but only to get the children here!' replied the Piper smiling.

'I don't understand! What's going on here?'

'It's quite simple Hopper, I am the Pied Piper!'

'That was just a story! He's not a real person!'

'He is real, and I am he,' said the Piper. 'All has gone according to my plan. You and Clint were instrumental in helping me. Clint's creation of the Hamelin rat was superb. He made them appear so real. And your ability to distract and lead the manhunt in the wrong direction was perfect. I thank you.'

'And so what now? You kill me too?' said Hopper.

'No, I like you. You may have been willing to do this terrible thing but I believe you have a good heart. Now go! Before I change my mind!'

At that, Hopper began to scramble over the rocks, away from the mouth of the cave, and then ran off.

'Run, run, run, as fast as you can! Or I'll shoot you in the back, you stupid ginger man!'

Hopper disappeared from view leaving the Piper with the children who were all visibly scared. Lucy didn't know what to do.

***

'I'm sorry children if I frightened you,' said the Piper with empathy on his face. 'Those two men were terrible individuals who wanted to hurt you. I brought you here to save you, and to take you to the most wonderful place in the world.'

The children began to relax a little, though some cast worried looks at the dead body of Clint still on the grass. The Piper stepped into the cave with the children and began to reload his pistol. He was then ready to begin the journey through the tunnel. He lifted his pipe to his lips, but before he blew one note, a shout came from outside the cave.

'Lucy! Lucy!'

The voice was that of Thomas. The Piper looked at Lucy who was about to respond. The Piper grabbed her around the mouth and whispered in her ear.

'If you want to see John again you better keep your mouth shut!'

Lucy nodded with fear in her eyes.

The Piper released her.

'Stay here children, I'll be back in a moment.'

The Piper stepped out of the cave to see Thomas arrive from around a cluster of trees.

'Where are they? Where's Lucy and the other children?'

'They're safe Thomas. Leave them be. I've rescued them from this world and will take them to a new world, a world of wonder.'

'Over my dead body!'

'That can be arranged,' said the Piper as he lifted his pistol and aimed it at Thomas.

'I don't want to shoot you, Thomas! Instead, come with me. There is a place there for you too! And your brother John is waiting for you!'

'John's dead!'

'He's not Thomas, he's very much alive. The children and I are going to join him. You should come too!'

'You're a liar and I'm not going anywhere with you, and neither are the children!'

'How are you going to stop me? I'm the one with the pistol!'

The Piper pulled back the hammer on his weapon.

'Drop it!' shouted Molly as she stepped out from behind a tree.

She had the flintlock in her hand, the one she had been looking after, and was pointing it at the Piper.

The Piper lowered his pistol gently releasing the hammer.

'Right on time young lady,' said the Piper.

'I said drop it, or I'll shoot! Said Molly.

The Piper tossed his pistol behind him and Molly moved to stand close to Thomas.

The Piper turned around and began to walk back toward the cave.

'Stop, or she'll shoot!' said Thomas.

The Piper stopped and spoke without turning round.

'She can't kill me, Thomas!'

'And why not,' he replied.

'Because killing me, would be the same as killing you!'

'What do you mean?'

'I mean Thomas that I am you! I'm you from a different time and place!'

The Piper began walking again but knew what was coming.

There was an explosion as Molly fired the flintlock. The Piper kept walking knowing he was not hit. He heard the sound of Thomas crying out and knew the lad was currently on the floor bleeding from the explosion. He also heard Molly scream.

Matthew Ryan

The Piper entered the cave leaving a bloody mess on the Brading Downs behind him. He began walking down the tunnel and within a few minutes, the entrance to the cave came crashing down sealing him and the children in.

'Let's go children. And be prepared for sights beyond your wildest dreams.

The Piper lifted his pipe to his lips once again, and the journey to paradise began.

PART 3

THE GARDEN

<u>Matthew Ryan</u>

CHAPTER 1

THOMAS & LUCY

Thomas staggered through the pitch black tunnel feeling his way as he went. His head was throbbing and his ears were still ringing from the explosion. Blood soaked the cloth that he had wrapped around his head as a bandage, and he was feeling more lightheaded with each step he took.

Lucy and the other children were long gone. They had followed the Piper deep into the cave and their singing, and the tune from the pipe hadn't been heard for some time.

Thomas stumbled and fell again, the fifth time in as many minutes. He felt more pain as rocks and stones dug into his knees and shins. He keeled over onto his side shaking and sweating. Lights were dancing in front of his eyes and the ringing in his ears continued. He lay where he was, collecting his thoughts, trying to control the pain he was feeling. He lay motionless letting the pain wash over him, and then began to try to understand what had just happened outside the cave.

First, was the revelation that John was alive, but was John really alive, or was this another lie spun by the Piper? Was this Piper chap that sick that he would take a poor defenceless boy and keep him captive in a cave? Surely not, but then there was the second revelation! The Piper said that he was him! A him from a different time and place, whatever that meant! The idea was ludicrous and completely impossible. Thomas had read many stories, especially from the good book, but he'd never heard anything like it. Thomas tried to dismiss the claim, but then remembered that the Piper had a terrible scar on the side of his face, and even had an ear missing. Thomas felt for his own ear, but could feel only blood and pain. It made his head swim and he felt on the verge of fainting.

'It's just a coincidence! It's just a coincidence!' he muttered to himself.

Thomas tried to stand but had to sit back down again. As he sat, he leaned his back against the cold stone wall and tried to see the object that he had in his hand. After the explosion from the flintlock, Molly had dropped it. Thomas picked it up as he staggered toward the cave. His mind had been a flurry of different thoughts and feelings but it felt right taking the weapon. The darkness prohibited him from seeing the flintlock and it's condition, so he tucked it away into his belt.

He began to think about Molly. He left his poor Molly on the other side! It pained him to think of her left behind, but he couldn't allow her into this nightmare. He had to keep her safe. No doubt she would get help so that he, his siblings, and the other children could escape.

Thomas sat for another few minutes trying to clear his head and work through the pain. He breathed deeply and licked his dry lips. He was exhausted but knew he needed to press on.

He stood, feeling very shaky, and put his hand on the rocky wall to his left to gain some balance. He began walking but staggered along slowly, feeling his way more carefully as he went. He thought about a verse in the good book as he walked, and kept repeating it over and over in his mind:

"Though I walk in the valley of deep shadow, I fear no harm,
For you are with me; Your rod and your staff reassure me."

Thomas walked for what felt like hours through the pitch-black tunnel.

Not only did the tunnel have many twists and turns, but also the tunnel was progressively going downward.

Thomas was starting to panic thinking that he would never catch up with Lucy or find her, but then he heard something that gave him hope.

He heard the sound of dripping water. He felt some relief not only because it was water, but also because he could hear. The ringing in his ears had slowly subsided but he was scared that the explosion from the flintlock had rendered him deaf. Thomas pushed on toward the sound of the dripping water. As he approached the sound, he could see light reflecting off a small pool. His eyes drank in the light and it gave his heart hope. The small pool was in a low alcove in the stone wall. Thomas stooped down and cupped some of the water with his hands. He sipped it slowly worrying that it would be foul or salty. It was, however, cool and fresh. Thomas took more handfuls of the water and eagerly drank it up. He splashed some on his face and felt a little better for doing so.

Thomas stood again and although he was in a lot of pain, he felt he could still press on. As he walked, Thomas looked to see if he could see the source of the light that he saw reflecting off the pool of water, and there it was. There was light at the end of the tunnel. The light was very small, almost like a pinprick. Thomas pushed on and his resolve was stronger than ever.

After what felt like several hours of staggering toward the light, Thomas felt extremely tired. The pinprick of light was now the size of a thumbnail, so Thomas decided to rest. He bent and slowly lowered himself to the floor. He then closed his eyes and rested. Sleep came quickly and his dreams were of Molly left alone outside.

He saw in his dream someone approach her from behind. A man in black, just like the Piper had been that first day he met him. Thomas called her name as the figure crept up on her, but she couldn't hear. The figure grabbed her.

Thomas woke sweating and panting. He felt very sore and his head felt heavy. After much difficulty, he was able to stand and begin walking again. He struggled on and on, walking toward the light. The end of the tunnel was getting closer and closer. The light that was the size of a thumbnail grew to the size of his palm, and then the size of a small child and before he knew it he was standing in a brightly lit doorway.

'I've made it!' Thomas said to himself.

Thomas stepped through the doorway and was shocked by what he saw on the other side.

***

Lucy's journey through the tunnel was very different from Thomas'. The journey that Thomas took felt to him like many hours or even days, but to Lucy, the journey felt like it lasted mere minutes.

Before the journey began, however, Lucy and the other children had been waiting for the Piper in the cave. There had been shouting outside and the Piper had threatened Lucy to be quiet. This scared Lucy, but she was desperate to see John again. So Lucy remained quiet, just as the Piper had instructed. Lucy had heard a commotion outside the cave, and a muffled conversation could be heard. It was while trying to listen to this that something strange happened. As she stood there, a pistol came tumbling into the cave. It landed mere feet from Lucy, and so Lucy picked it up. The pistol was similar to the flintlock she had stolen from the Folly Tower. This pistol, however, was jet black and lighter to hold. She heard steps as the Piper returned and so quickly tucked the pistol in her belt and covered it with her jerkin.

The Piper returned to the children with tears in his eyes. He tried to hide it, but Lucy saw it clearly. Within seconds, the sad Piper was full of joy and excitement again.

'Are you ready to see wonders children, beyond your wildest of dreams?' said the Piper.

All the children cheered in excitement.

'Then let's go!'

At that, the Piper took out his pipe once again, played his tune, and danced as he played. He led the children deeper into the cave and tunnel, and they all happily followed him.

The tunnel had several twists and turns but was well lit by candles up above, near the arched stone ceiling. As the Piper went past each candle, however, the

flame blew out. When Lucy looked back all she could see was darkness. This should have scared her but she was happy listening to the Piper play his merry tune and trusted him to lead her to John.

There was a moment during the journey when they stopped for a few minutes. In an alcove nearby was a pool of water around the size of a feeding trough. The Piper encouraged them to drink and refresh themselves, which they all gladly did. As soon as everyone was ready, they were off again on their journey.

Within a few minutes, they reached an open doorway with light beaming through. The light was very bright and made it difficult to see, but still, the Piper continued on and all the children followed. As soon, as Lucy, stepped through the doorway, however, her eyes adjusted and she could see that the light actually came from the sun. She looked about and saw a sight like nothing she had ever seen before.

Lucy saw hills, mountains, and rivers. She saw fruit trees of every kind, and there were animals as well. There were birds flying in the sky. There were dogs, cats, and rats. There were cows, horses, and pigs. And even lions, tigers, and bears. There were also small cottages scattered about and a large wooden cabin on a hill. The place was more than just beautiful, it was paradise.

The Piper continued playing his pipe and led them dancing across one of the meadows. He took them toward a river and over a wooden bridge. He then led them up a hill toward the large wooden cabin. Various animals approached the children as they danced along. The animals approached without fear and even the children were not scared. Lucy stroked a white tiger that had bounded toward her. The tiger lay on its back and she rubbed its stomach. It was truly amazing. The children continued following the Piper as he led them up the wooden steps to the entrance of the cabin. As the man approached, the double doors swung open for them all. Lucy and the other children went into the building.

Inside the wooden cabin, it was surprising to see that it was one big room. Lucy thought that it was similar in size to the church in Brading. There were also pews, that the children all began to sit on. Lucy picked a spot and sat like

the others in the room waiting eagerly for what was going to happen next. She watched as the Piper continued playing his pipe and moved to the front of the room. The Piper stopped playing his pipe, mounted a stage, and then turned to the children.

'Welcome to the garden! The garden of Eden!'

CHAPTER 2

JOHN & THE PIPER

It was early morning and the sun was just beginning to peak above the trees to the East of the garden. There was a layer of dew on the grass that glittered in the morning light.

John awoke to the sound of birds singing and sat up in good spirits feeling refreshed and fully rested. Despite sleeping in the long grass under the same tree every night since his arrival, he never woke in discomfort. His sleep was always deep, perfect, and refreshing.

John stood and began to walk toward the main river that ran through the garden. He felt the cool droplets of the dew on the grass against his bare feet and it felt nice.

A smile was spread across his face. It still amazed him that he could walk. The days of being a cripple were long gone and John didn't miss a thing about it. The Piper had saved him and freed him from his infirmity.

He remembered vividly that day that he nearly died.

John remembered falling from the window of the house in Brading. It was as if time had slowed down as he fell. He remembered clearly the pain he felt when he hit the floor. He felt bones breaking all over his body. He remembered struggling to breathe as if his lungs were not working properly. He saw in his mind's eye the rats bounding toward him with mouths open ready to tear the flesh from his bones, but then the man dressed in black appeared causing the rats to flee. The man dressed in black bent down and lifted him up and John remembered the smell of tobacco on the man's clothing. John also remembered falling asleep as he was carried away and awakening in a dark stone room where he was given water to drink. He remembered sleeping again and then waking up in the garden. The Piper was bathing John's legs in the river and encouraged him to drink the cool refreshing water.

He remembered what the Piper had said as he drank.

'Your sins are forgiven! Stand and walk young John!'

And John did. He stood and walked, and ran, and jumped, and even danced. It was the happiest moment of his life and he owed it all to the Piper.

After being cured, John began to explore his new home. The garden was a beautiful place, a true paradise on earth. John explored the forests and fields, and even climbed high hilltops and descended into deep ravines.

It was during one of these walks that John was passing through a dense woodland area when he suddenly entered a clearing. There was a low hill, with the river running by next to it, and on the hill stood a lone tree. The tree was unlike any tree that John had ever seen before. In the garden was an abundance of trees and fruits, but this tree was completely different.

The bark of the tree itself was dark brown in colour, and the trunk and branches were thick and appeared very strong. Even the roots appeared thick and deep. The leaves of the tree were a mixture of colours. Some were a golden yellow while others were a deep green with a purple edging.

It was the fruit itself that John was drawn to. The fruit was similar in shape to a pear but appeared to have the texture of an orange. The colour of the fruit was a deep scarlet and it looked enticing. John began to move toward it. He wanted to touch the fruit and pick it and taste it. He reached out to pluck a piece of the fruit from the tree.

'I wouldn't do that if I were you!'

John remembered pulling his hand back in shock. The Piper stepped out of the trees into the clearing. He then began to walk up the hill toward him with his hands tucked into the crook of his back.

'What is this tree? It's very different to all the others I've seen,' asked John.

'It is the tree that Eve ate from. The tree that has brought a curse on the whole of mankind!'

John remembered looking at the tree and suddenly feeling scared. It was as if a thousand cold fingers were running up his back. He shivered in response.

'How do you know that?' asked John.

'Take a piece of fruit and eat it! You'll know for sure then! Your heart would immediately turn to stone in your chest. Your ribs would begin to tighten and restrict you from breathing. You would claw at your throat trying to draw breath, and just before you blacked out you'd notice your finger and hands begin to turn to dust. Try it and see!'

John stepped back away from the tree and its enticing fruit.

'I've seen it too many times,' said the Piper. 'Someone sees the fruit and can't resist it. Within a few minutes, they become a pile of dust that is quickly blown away by the wind! Come, let us not linger on this hill, Let us walk and talk.'

The Piper then walked back to the middle of the garden with John, telling him all about his garden of Eden.

That was several days ago. Since then the Piper had left and had promised a surprise for John when he returned. While the Piper was gone, John explored the garden more and found that there was a boundary to the garden. The garden, though gigantic in size, was surrounded by a wall of thorns and thistles. The wall was so thick with brambles and other nasty plants that John could not see beyond it. Despite the boundary, John thought the garden was a truly wonderful place. He loved playing with the animals and swimming in the river. He loved eating the various fruits and vegetables and loved feeling truly at peace.

There was one thing, however, that John didn't like. He didn't like being alone. He missed his family and wondered where they all were and what they were doing. He missed Will and Alice too. He even missed aunt Emmy and hoped she was safe.

John was lost in these thoughts, but then suddenly he heard a sound that he hadn't heard for a long time. It was the sound of children laughing.

***

It's done! thought the Piper as he slumped into his rickety old chair.

He pulled out one of his cigars from his inside pocket and lit it with a candle that was on his desk.

They just need a day or two to acclimatise and then they'll be ready to start working. Hopefully, they will last longer than the last group.

The Piper was happy that this part of his plan had run pretty smoothly but he was concerned with what happened with Thomas. Events did not play out quite as they should have and it appeared that Thomas was not the one he had been waiting for after all.

He can't be! He's now laying outside the cave either dead or dying.

This worried the Piper as he knew that he had only a short time left to live and no replacement had appeared. Time was short. He planned to rest up for a few days and help the children to settle before their service began. Then he planned to head back out and into a new town where his replacement may be found.

The Piper stood and began to take off his hat and coat. As he did so, a thought came to mind.

Have I left too many witnesses? He thought. *There's not only Thomas Smith, but also the girl and the ginger man.*

There was silence as the Piper paced. The only sound that could be heard was the sound of the Piper's booted feet against the Wooden floor. The Piper glanced around the room as he paced. The walls were filled from top to bottom with books. The books were not stacked neatly on shelves like those in a library but rather were stacked in piles on the floor reaching high to the ceiling. There didn't appear to be any order to the books either. They were stacked randomly one on top of the other. On one wall there hung a large picture of a garden with various animals at play. On the opposite wall hung a large mirror.

I don't need to worry about the ginger man! He'll take the fall for the crime, that's why I let him go. Thomas Smith is probably bleeding to death, so will unlikely be able to tell anyone anything. And let's be honest, who is going to believe a delirious girl?

In theory, all would be fine.

The Piper walked over to the mirror and looked at himself.

If it becomes a problem then I'll deal with it!

The Piper's thoughts were disturbed by a barrage of squeaking that came from behind him. The Piper could see the squeaking rat sitting on his desk behind him, through the mirror.

'Repeat that again,' said the Piper.

The rat squeaked some more but more slowly.

'So we have an intruder!' said the Piper out loud, smiling to himself.

CHAPTER 3

THE CAPTAIN & MOLLY

Captain Campion strode through Brading Town toward Gunne House. A thick fog had descended upon the town, and the smell of smoke from the fire of three nights ago still lingered in the air. Several searches had been carried out to find the children, but there was no sign of them or the Piper anywhere. That was until around 6 o'clock that morning when a man had been reprimanded. He had been caught trying to board a ship at the Havens. A ship Captain had engaged with the man and found him to be completely delirious. The Captain bound the man, and then took him to one of the local guards. The guard in turn had brought him to Brading. The Captain was extremely eager to speak to this man.

The Captain entered the room in Gunne House where the man was to be questioned. Sargent Carruthers was already there with a guard keeping watch. The Captain looked at the man. He looked as if he were in his early twenties. He had shoulder-length ginger hair and a short unkempt beard. His clothes were filthy as if he'd been crawling through mud. He was fiddling with the chains that bound his wrists.

'Guard, you can leave us,' said the Captain.

The guard left the room.

'Has he said anything yet Sargent?'

'He just keeps repeating that it wasn't him.'

'It wasn't me!' said the man. 'I had nothing to do with it!'

'Nothing to do with what?' said the Captain, as he sat down opposite the man.

'The children! It wasn't me!'

'Where are the children?'

'I don't know! It's nothing to do with me! I'm completely innocent in this!'

The man was becoming more agitated. His eyes were like wild horses, darting around everywhere. He was nervous and was twitching uncontrollably.

'I'm sure you are innocent my good man and I'm sure this is all a mistake.'

'It is! It is!'

'What's your name, my friend?'

'It's Hopper, Matt Hopper.'

'Mr Hopper, we're here to help. So tell us what you know.'

'But that's what I'm telling you, I don't know anything!'

Sargent Carruthers whispered to the Captain. Hopper shifted uncomfortably in his chair and began to bite his nails.

'My informed colleague has told me that you were one of the rat catchers that were working here,' said the Captain. 'Is that true?'

'Er....yes, I was....but....'

'Yes, I remember you now. You were one of the men that found the Hamelin rat!'

'That wasn't my idea. That was Brady and Clint!'

'What wasn't your idea?'

'The rat! I thought it was stupid but they said it would work!'

'Mr Hopper, this is all very confusing! I think it would be best if you were to start at the beginning. How did you know Mr Brady and Mr Clint?'

'I've worked for Clint as a rat catcher for the past year. Before that, I was a baker. Brady approached us in a tavern in Lower Ryde. He said that he knew of a rat infestation and that he was the only one who could get rid of them, but he needed help. He promised us a grand reward for helping, and so we did!'

'Did you bring the rats?'

'No! It was nothing to do with me! Whenever I asked questions they would say "Shut up Hopper!" and that was all they kept saying. Every time I found it hard to watch the bad things that were happening they would goad me, "Run, run, run, as fast as you can!"'

'What happened to Mr Brady and Mr Clint?'

Hopper suppressed a tear.

'Brady took the children and shot Clint!'

Tears began to well up in Hopper's eyes.

'Why didn't Mr Brady shoot you?'

'I don't know!'

'Because you were part of it, weren't you?'

'No, it was nothing to do with me!'

'If I could just interject Captain, Sir. Wasn't it you Mr Hopper who approached us at the Western watchtower that night? You ran to tell us that the Piper had taken the children and gone South?'

'Er.....No....That wasn't....'

'Yes! That's right,' interrupted the Captain. 'You sent us the wrong way so that the Piper could get away with the children!'

'You helped kidnap the children, didn't you?' said the Sargent.

'No.....no....'

'Where did they go?' said the Captain getting angry.

'The Brading Downs, now please let me go!'

The Captain stood.

'Guard!'

The guard entered the room.

'Arrange for Mr Hopper to be held in custody. I want a guard continually stationed outside the lockup!'

'Yes Sir,' replied the guard.

Hopper began to sob hysterically.

'No......please......I had nothing to do with it!'

The guard moved over to Hopper and hoisted him to his feet. He then dragged him out of the room kicking and screaming. The Captain stood and went to a nearby writing bureau. He sat down and began to write a letter.

'That was excellent work Carruthers. You identified him well despite the dark that evening,' said the Captain as he wrote.

'Thank you, Captain.'

'We need to get to Brading Downs. Gather some guards.'

'Yes sir,' replied Carruthers. 'What are you doing?'

'I'm sending for help!'

***

It was the third day since Thomas and the children had gone into the cave. The trail of Thomas' blood could still be seen leading to where the entrance had once been. Molly sat on a log opposite the rocky wall. Her red cloak was wrapped tightly around her, but she was still shivering from the cold wind that was blowing over the Brading Downs. She sang softly to herself to keep her mind occupied as she waited.

The dead body of Clint still lay face down a few yards away from her. The smell of his decomposing body filled her nostrils but didn't appear to faze her. She sat waiting expectantly for Thomas and the others to return.

At first, Molly had been at a loss thinking of what to do. After Thomas went into the cave it sealed shut and she didn't know how it happened.

One minute there was the cave, and then she heard a loud crash, and then there were only rocks. Molly had tried to pull the rocks away to open the cave entrance again, but it was too difficult for her. The larger stones would not budge and she bloodied her hands in the attempt.

Molly had thought about taking a horse and going back to town for help, but she was scared that the cave might open again and she miss it, or that Thomas might come back and she not be there. And so Molly resigned herself to waiting, hoping that the cave would open again soon.

Molly hadn't eaten or drunk, or even slept, since the incident happened and so was malnourished and dehydrated. In fact, Molly was in such a bad state that when she was found, she at first didn't even notice. From the corner of her eye, she saw a guard come into view, heard him blow his whistle, and then come running toward her. She remained focussed on the rocks and where the cave had been. Even when the guard grabbed her by the shoulders and was trying to talk to her, she still stared intently at the wall. It wasn't until she felt several hands grab hold of her, and try to pull her away, that she finally realised that help had arrived.

Molly felt a flash of relief pass over her.

Molly, It's all going to be fine, she thought. *You need to rest. Sleep. Just sleep.*

Molly passed out knowing that now there was help, she would see her beloved Thomas again.

CHAPTER 4

JOHN & THOMAS

John stood looking at Lucy who was with the group of other children. His sister looked as if she had grown taller since he had last seen her. John saw many of the other children from the town, including Will and Alice. It warmed his heart to see them again too. Lucy saw him and froze in shock. John ran toward her and hugged her tight.

'John? Is it really you?'

'It's me'

'But you're walking!'

'It was the Piper, he healed me!'

'I don't understand! Where have you been?

'It's a long story. We can talk later. Come.'

The two began to walk arm in arm. John noticed that Lucy was looking around at the paradise garden.

'What is this place?' she asked.

'Didn't the Piper explain?'

'Yes, he said it's the garden of Eden. Is it really so?'

'Yes,' John replied with a smile on his face.

'I've never seen anything like it?'

'Apparently, very few have. Oh, Lucy, there is so much to tell you!'

'I've missed you, John.'

'I've missed you too.' He replied. 'Tell me of Thomas. Is he safe and well?'

'Yes, I think so. So much has happened and I have so much to tell you!'

'We have a lot to catch up on. You must tell me everything.'

'Where are you taking me?' she asked.

'To a little grove which I call home. Do you see it?'

John pointed to a small cluster of trees in the distance.

'Yes, I see it, It looks good.'

The two continued on arm in arm.

'John, Is there a way out of this place?' she asked.

'No, why?'

'We need to get out of here. The Piper is dangerous! I don't trust him!'

'He saved my life, and yours too!' he replied sternly.

'No John, he's an imposter. He kidnapped the children and lured them here!'

John recalled that the Piper had said, during one of their many chats, that others would come who would not believe the truth, but he told John that he needed to be patient with these ones.

'Please Lucy, give it some time and listen to what the Piper has to say. Everything will make perfect sense. Remember what Christ said in the good book, he said: "you will know the truth, and the truth will set you free." He will set you free Lucy, just as he did me.'

'You've changed John.'

'I know, and so will you! Just think, all we've ever wanted was a place to call home and I think this could be it!'

John felt elated, he was in the most perfect place in the world and he wanted Lucy to feel the same too. Lucy was still adjusting but he believed she would be fine.

The two continued on and John pointed out various things along the way and told Lucy of all the wonderful things he had done since being in the garden.

After, around twenty minutes of walking, the two arrived at the grove of trees.

***

Thomas stood looking at the vast cavern in front of him where the light looked almost as bright as day. His eyes took several moments to adjust after the pitch blackness of the tunnel. The size of the cavern was enormous.

You could fit the whole of Brading in this place! said Thomas to himself.

As Thomas looked about the cavern he saw several wooden buildings and a few shacks scattered throughout the large area. It was almost like a village. Thomas also saw a river flowing through the cavern with a wooden bridge extending over the widest part. At the furthest end of the cavern, stood on a hill of rock, was what appeared to be a lighthouse. The light at the top of the lighthouse lit up the whole cavern.

What on earth is a lighthouse doing underground? Thomas thought

Thomas knew that the Piper would be there, so he gathered his strength and pushed on. He walked toward the bridge so as to cross it to reach the lighthouse, but decided first to head toward the nearest building to see what it was and if anyone was inside.

As Thomas approached the building, he saw that it was a barn and that the doors were open. He peeked inside and saw mountains of foodstuffs. There was fresh fruit and vegetables. There were salted fresh fish, barrels of water, and various alcoholic beverages. There were also small barrels of tobacco and cases of the thin brown objects the Piper liked to smoke.

Where did it all come from? thought Thomas. *And why is it here?*

Thomas tasted the water and it tasted good. It tasted just like the water from the river Yar. Thomas drank the water and ate some fruit, and felt better for doing so. As he sat eating and drinking, a rat scuttled into the barn. Thomas froze wondering if it would attack, or sound an alarm to other rats nearby, but the rat simply looked at him and scurried off again. Thomas continued eating and used the opportunity to examine the flintlock. He pulled the weapon from his belt and looked over it. The barrel of the pistol had blackened from when Molly had fired it. Having never handled a pistol before, he didn't know if its condition was normal. He briefly looked around the barn

to see if there was anything he could reload the flintlock with, but unfortunately found nothing. Thomas wiped his mouth on his sleeve, tucked the pistol away, and decided to continue on toward the lighthouse.

Thomas continued walking and checked a few of the other buildings along the way. One was like a tavern but completely empty inside. One reminded Thomas of an orphanage. It was filled with rows upon rows of beds, with storage chests at the foot of each one. Another building was filled with tables and chairs, and another contained a large rowboat. Thomas decided to leave some of the other buildings unexplored and press on toward the lighthouse.

He reached the wooden bridge that hung over the river. It looked old but strong. Thomas tested each step as he went and managed to cross without incident.

He continued on toward the lighthouse but as he approached he saw a very disturbing sight. The lighthouse was surrounded by large piles of skeletons. Many are the skulls and bones were of animals, mostly rats, but there were also many human skulls. Some appeared to be that of children and even skulls of adults were seen too. As Thomas walked, he began to feel physically sick and tears stung his eyes.

Please God, let the children be safe.

He was about to begin walking through the pile of skeletons when suddenly he heard laughter. The laughter was like that of a child. The laughter came again and so Thomas turned away from the lighthouse and followed the sound. He walked down a rocky slope being careful not to slip. As he walked he heard more laughter and saw in the distance what appeared to be a group of children sitting in a circle with a pile of stones in the middle. Relief flooded through his body and he began to run toward them. As he ran he could hear them singing Pat-a-Cake and clapping their hands against one another. Thomas ran hoping that it was Lucy and the other children.

As he reached them he saw that they were all laughing and talking, but none of them saw him or even heard him approach. Thomas saw that each child was dirty and bloodied, and wore shackles around their ankles. Thomas saw one child, one of John's friends, pick up a small rock and bite into it like it was an apple. Thomas saw a few of the boy's teeth break and then blood spill from the child's mouth, but still, the boy laughed and ate. Thomas moved into the circle of children trying to find his sister. As he searched he found her sitting with a skinny boy. The boy looked close to death.

'Lucy!' shouted Thomas.

She didn't hear him! Thomas moved closer and saw the face of the boy she was talking to.

'John!' he cried out.

It was at that moment that Thomas' head suddenly hurt. Something had hit him, and then everything went black.

CHAPTER 5

THE PIPER & LUCY

Thomas lay on the floor of the cell that the rats had carried him to. The Piper felt a touch of guilt having hit Thomas on the head with a rock. The boy had already suffered damage to his head from the explosion of the pistol, and now he would feel even worse. The Piper wiped the fresh blood away from Thomas' wound with some clean rags and worked at stopping the bleeding, but something was wrong with the situation.

It isn't supposed to happen this way, he thought.

The Piper considered his own journey of discovery when he entered this place. He remembered the revelation at the entrance to the cave and remembered the Piper's invitation to join him. He remembered accepting the invitation and being shot by the girl who was trying to save him. That shot had cost him his ear. He remembered following the Piper and the children into the cave, and then the cavern. However, he remembered walking into the cavern and seeing paradise. He remembered seeing the children laughing and playing. He even remembered joining in the merriment himself.

He also remembered his discussion with his future self about taking over as the Piper. He knew that he had been sceptical, but he agreed to learn and that's what he did. He learned everything he needed to learn and completely understood what had to be done and why. After his future self had died, he was ready to take over.

The Piper

Everything that had happened with Thomas so far had been the same but now it was different and the Piper didn't understand why. His future self had said that one day someone would come to continue the work and surely Thomas was the one. He had to be.

The Piper looked at Thomas as he worked on his wounds.

'What's happening Thomas? Why are you even here? Is it because you truly are the one I've been looking for?'

Thomas remained still, breathing lightly.

'You should have just joined me when I offered you the chance, and now you're badly injured! I had plans for you to replace me! To learn everything and carry on in our crusade!

We are destined to die an eternal death but we can save the children! We can help them to gain everlasting life in paradise. They can't live in a world as rotten as this. They deserve better, and we have a chance to give that to them!

The Piper continued to work on Thomas' wounds. He stopped those that were bleeding and then cleaned his cuts and bruises with fresh water and clean rags. The Piper then began to apply new bandages to the more serious wounds and began to pray for the boy's recovery. After finishing, the Piper locked shackles around Thomas' ankles but the boy still did not stir.

The Piper walked toward the cell door leaving Thomas laying still on the floor. He stood in the doorway and looked back at Thomas.

'Such a pity!' said the Piper.

The Piper then shut the door and left.

Thomas opened his eyes.

***

Matthew Ryan

Lucy had spent the last few days of her time in the garden exploring and thinking. She had been manipulated by the Piper into following him to this place, and despite his reasons, she did not trust him. It was true that she was reunited with John, and it was true that the garden was a beautiful place. It was also true that their sicknesses and infirmities were cured, and that everyone was living in peace. But Lucy still did not trust the Piper.

Lucy tried to find some evidence that things were not right. She examined the trees and the fruits. She examined the plants and the animals. She even examined the grass and the rocks. Lucy never found anything out of the ordinary. It wasn't until she examined the river that she found something not quite right.

The river was the only source of water in the garden. It was an absolutely beautiful river in every sense, but one thing was wrong, the water didn't taste right. It didn't taste bad, just not right. Lucy called to mind the water in Brading. It was the most refreshing water on the island and tasted good, but this water didn't taste as nice. This began to bother Lucy. If this was the garden of Eden and was paradise like the Piper claimed, then surely the water would taste even better than the water in Brading. This bothered Lucy to such a degree that she decided to investigate it. Her aim was to try to ascertain why the water tasted so strange and so Lucy began her investigation by following the river. Her following the river led her to the forbidden tree where the river ran close to it.

The Piper had warned the children about the tree. He had told them to never eat from the tree, not to even touch the fruit, or they would die. As she approached the tree, Lucy was immediately drawn to it and its fruit. She pulled her gaze away from the tree and tried to focus on the task at hand.

She knelt down by the river and tasted the water nearest the tree and immediately spat it back out. It tasted bad, almost like chalk. Despite spitting the water out she felt a reaction to the water. It made her feel dizzy and nauseous. Her stomach began to cramp causing her to grab her belly. She retched but nothing came out. She crawled away from the river toward the shade of the large forbidden tree. She lay on the cool grass waiting for the pain to pass.

Lucy lay for a long time waiting for the pain to subside. As the worst of the pain passed, she sat up and wiped the sweat from her forehead with her sleeve. She stood feeling very shaky and moved toward the river again. The water was clear allowing her to see the riverbed. Nothing out of the ordinary appeared to be there but she assumed that the tree with the strange fruit was possibly polluting the water.

Lucy decided to follow the river further upstream to see if there was any other possible reason for the water being foul. Within a hundred yards Lucy reached a large wall of brambles that she could not pass through. The brambles were so thick that she couldn't even see through them to the other side.

What's beyond the brambles? she thought. *Maybe it's a way out of the garden!*

CHAPTER 6

LUCY & JOHN

It was two days after refusing to drink the water from the river that Lucy began to hallucinate. After learning that something was wrong with the water, Lucy decided to stop drinking it. Lucy also tried to avoid eating anything in case it too was contaminated.

The first hallucination occurred after her stroll during the breezy part of the day. While walking, Lucy began to feel very lightheaded. She assumed that it was because she hadn't drank for some time and so stopped for a rest. Lucy proceeded to sit on the grass but as soon as she slumped down, she wasn't sitting on grass, it was stone. It felt so strange. She could see the grass, could even smell it, but when she touched it she felt stone. Her heart began to beat fast and she began to sweat. She heard a noise behind her, a scraping of metal on stone, and so spun around. A rocky wall stood in front of her. The rocks of the wall were cracked and had moss growing from the crevices.

What's going on? she thought to herself.

She rubbed her eyes and was then suddenly back in the garden again. The grass felt soft between her fingers and her dizziness passed. The experience worried Lucy but still, she refused to drink the water.

The second hallucination occurred later that same day. Lucy was with John sitting by a fire, as they did every night. One minute she was looking at him sitting with a smile on his face in the best of health, the

next he was gone. He was replaced by a very different John, a very frail and sick-looking John. The
smile was still there on his face, but he looked hollow and pale. Again, she rubbed her eyes and the vision was gone.

'What's wrong?' John asked. 'You looked as if you were just daydreaming!'

Lucy shook her head.

'I think I did.' She replied confused. 'It's the second time it's happened!'

'What's happened?'

'The feeling that I'm dreaming or that I'm not quite here!'

'I'm confused,' said John. 'Explain.'

'Earlier today, I was walking along, going for my daily stroll before we started gardening. All of a sudden I felt dizzy and lightheaded, and so I sat down. Instead of sitting on grass, I felt as if I were sitting on stone!'

'What do you mean you felt like you were sitting on stone? Obviously, you must have been!'

'No! I was sitting on grass but it didn't feel like grass, it felt like stone! And then I heard a noise and turned around and saw a stone wall.'

'A stone wall? There are no stone walls here!'

'Precisely!'

'So what happened just now?' he asked.

'I was looking at you and then I saw a different you. A sick you. A you that was close to death!'

'That's very strange! What do you think's causing it?'

'I think it's the water. I think there's something wrong with it.'

'The water tastes fine to me.' John responded. 'Should I go to find the Piper and ask him about it?'

'No, it's fine. I'm sure you're right and I'm just daydreaming. Maybe I'm just overtired and missing Thomas.' Lucy lied.

'I'm sure you're right! Let's get some sleep. It sounds like you need it,' John laughed.

Lucy laughed too.

'You're right.'

The two began to get ready to sleep in the small grove. John fell asleep almost immediately, but Lucy lay for several hours awake worrying.

***

John awoke early with the sun just beginning to peek over the far horizon. Lucy was still asleep and so John left her snoring in the small grove of trees. John planned to meet up with Will and Alice but hoped that he would see the Piper first. He hadn't seen him for a few days and this began to worry him. The Piper had been good to him and John felt that he owed the Piper his life. Lucy had previously expressed a different view of the Piper, but that was to be expected. The Piper warned him of this. John wanted to prove to Lucy that the Piper was a good man. He wasn't sure how he was going to do it but knew he needed to.

John decided to take a stroll before he met up for breakfast with his friends. He decided to check out the work that was being done by the children to build little cabins to live in. Since arriving, the children had been sleeping under trees and by the riverbank and needed places more comfortable to sleep. John himself still slept in his little grove of trees but he liked it that way.

The walk was fantastic and gave John a wonderful sense of well-being. The sun was shining and the smell of flowers in the air was beautiful. He saw several of the animals lazing in the long grass together. It reminded him of words from the good book:

The wolf will reside for a while with the lamb,
And with the young goat the leopard will lie down,
And the calf and the lion and the fattened animal will all be together;
And a little boy will lead them.
The cow and the bear will feed together,
And their young will lie down together.
The lion will eat straw like the bull.

All the animals appeared to be at peace and it truly was a wonderful sight to behold. He was so thankful to the Piper for bringing him to the garden and hoped that he could live there in peace forever.

After around twenty minutes of walking, John arrived at the area where the children had been working. They had made progress in cutting down a few trees and stripping them of their leaves and branches. It amazed him that despite many of the children being young that they could do such hard work. The garden truly was an amazing place. It not only cured you of your diseases and ailments but also made you stronger and wiser. All this was thanks to the Piper.

After looking over the progress made, John walked back to join his friends for breakfast with that wonderful sense of wellbeing still in his heart.

CHAPTER 7

THOMAS & THE PIPER

Thomas sat at a table in front of the Piper. His head ached and he felt a lot of pain in his ankles where shackles had been secured to him. His body was covered in bruises and cuts from his trip through the tunnel but at least he had stopped bleeding. The Piper picked up a goblet from the table and poured water into it from a jug. The Piper then slid the goblet across to Thomas.

'Have a drink,' said the Piper. 'It'll make you feel better.'

'I'm not drinking that! It's probably poison.'

The Piper picked up the goblet and took a mouthful.

'It's just water, Thomas. I want to help you not harm you.'

The Piper saw Thomas look at the goblet and again slid it over to him. Thomas lifted the goblet and took a small mouthful. He then quickly guzzled down the rest. The Piper picked up the nearby jug and poured Thomas another cupful. Thomas drank deeply again. Within a few minutes, Thomas began to feel somewhat better. He felt renewed and more alert.

'I'm so glad you're here Thomas!' said the Piper 'There's so much I need to talk about with you.'

'I'm not here to talk to you! I'm here for my brother and sister, and the other children. Release me now or I swear I'll kill you!'

'It would be like killing yourself!' replied the Piper. 'I told you before that I am you. I'm you from a different time and place.'

The Piper

'You're completely insane!' said Thomas.

'Listen for a moment Thomas and I shall tell you a strange tale. It's my story, or should I say our story.'

Thomas sat and listened to the Piper's tale.

'I was sixteen and lived with my family. One day, my family and I were forced to leave the village we were living in, and so we moved to a new town. Within a short time, a great multitude of events happened. Rats invaded the town, my mother was murdered, my father was taken prisoner, my siblings disappeared, and I fell in love. Then a strange man appeared in the town. He saved the town from the rats, but the townsfolk refused to pay him. And so the stranger took the children from the town.'

Thomas opened his mouth to speak but the Piper raised a hand in objection.

'I pursued the stranger to a cave where he revealed that he was me. He invited me to join him and leave my old life behind. I agreed but my true love pursued us and accidentally injured me in the pursuit. The Piper saved me and healed me. He then taught me everything he knew and trained me to take over as the Piper.'

'So that's what you did?' said Thomas.

'Yes.'

'And you want me to do the same, take over from you?'

'It's your destiny Thomas, you can't escape it!'

'What happens to the children that are taken?

'They are eventually taken to paradise!'

'Eventually?'

'Yes, they need to pay for the sins of their parents first , and then they'll wake up in paradise.'

'How do they pay for the sins of their parents?'

'With servitude. They serve me here in my kingdom and when they die they will wake in paradise!'

'When they die?' said Thomas. 'You mean that you kill them?'

'No, no Thomas my boy. They die themselves, normally from starvation or disease but they won't feel a thing. They're mentally in a special place where they feel no pain!'

'What kind of sick person are you? How can you do such a thing?'

'Thomas, it's for their own good. I'm actually saving their lives. They will awaken in a new world where they will live forever in true peace and security.'

Thomas sat in silence trying to piece together everything he had heard. Were all the skulls that he had seen around the base of the lighthouse all those that had previously served him? Were they all now in paradise? Thomas didn't want to know the answer.

'Why didn't you tell me from the start who you were?' asked Thomas.

'I had to play it out exactly as it happened to me. I had to tell you at the right moment.'

'So how did you manage to travel through time? If that's what you call it.'

'Unfortunately Thomas, that I don't know. I travel through the various tunnels playing my pipe and each time, I arrive somewhere new. I was told that one day I would travel to my past and would meet myself. I was told to train my younger self to become the new Piper so that the wheel can keep on turning.'

'So the pipe you play, has it got some kind of power?' asked Thomas.

'Again I don't know. I was never taught how to play the pipe, it just came naturally. I was taught, however, how to control the songs I played and use them to control others. I'm not sure if the pipe is powerful itself. I've never thought so, but rather have always believed that the power comes from me!

'But....'

'Look, Thomas, you have dozens if not hundreds of questions and I will help you to find the answers to them all. All I'm asking is that you give me a chance. There is so much I need to tell you and teach you, but time is short. What do you say?'

Thomas thought deeply.

The Piper stood up and began to pace the cell. Thomas could see that he was visibly agitated. Thomas answered.

'No! I would rather die!'

'Thomas, it's your fate! You're destined to be me!'

'No! Never! If what you say is true then I'll be the one to break the pattern!'

'You stupid boy!' said the Piper angry.

The Piper stormed off out of the cell, locking the door behind him.

***

The Piper sat with his head in his hands musing over his map. He massaged his temples and stared absently at the large drawing in front of him.

'Why won't the boy listen to me?' he said to himself out loud. 'I don't recall ever being as thick-headed as he is. When I was offered the same opportunity I took it! Never once did I say no!'

The Piper stood from the table pushing his chair back with such force that the chair toppled over. He strode across the room to a large rickety cupboard and swung its doors open. Inside were various ornaments and trinkets including bones, jewellery, and even a live frog in a small tank. The Piper reached into the cupboard and grabbed a large brown bottle with a cork sticking out. He gripped the cork between his teeth, pulled it out, and then spat the cork onto the floor. The Piper then took several gulps of the liquid and put the bottle on the table. He then began to pace up and down the room.

'Think! What can I do to convince him? Think!'

He picked up the bottle again and took another mouthful as he walked.

'What motivates a man? Money? Power? Threats? Some, maybe even most, but not Thomas! He is driven by love. Love for his family and love for his girl! That's the motivation, I need to use his love for them to break him! I have his siblings already but if I also had the girl then that would fully motivate him! What was her name?'

The Piper drank more from his bottle as he paced.

'Molly! That's it, the girls name was Molly!'

The Piper smiled and then took another swig from his bottle. Plans were beginning to hatch in his mind. Thomas would be his!

CHAPTER 8

THE CAPTAIN & MOLLY

The Captain had been overseeing the excavation of where the cave entrance had been. Despite hiring some of the best miners on the Wyght Island, and having them work night and day for two solid days, there had been no breakthrough. Sargent Carruthers stood next to the Captain who was currently smoking his pipe and in deep thought.

'What are you thinking, Captain?'

'I'm thinking Carruthers, that we are searching in the wrong place.'

'I don't understand Captain. After all, that Molly girl was here sitting opposite the entrance and there is the trail of blood leading to where the men are working. Surely this is the right place to search!'

'That is true my learned friend but there is more to this.'

'Do you mean magic, Captain?'

'There is no such thing Sargent, but our Piper friend wants us to believe that there is. Take for example the wagon over there that the criminals used. Did you take a look at what was inside the storage chest it was hauling?'

'Yes, the chest was filled with those Hamelin rat things. They were fake. They looked real from a distance but up close they look ridiculous!'

'Yes Carruthers, they do. Examining them closely from the start would have uncovered the lies that have been told, but the men used fear in order to stop us from taking a closer look.'

'What's that got to do with them wanting us to believe in magic?' asked Carruthers.

'It's all a ruse. It's simply trickery and deception. Come, I want to show you something.'

The Captain walked toward where the men were working and the Sargent followed. As the two men approached, the workers stopped digging and went to have a short water break. The Captain picked up a stone from where the men had been working and showed it to the Sargent.

'Can you see what's on this stone Sargent?'

Sargent Carruthers took the stone and examined it. There was a chalky substance over it.

'It's either dirt or dust Captain. Maybe even dark chalk.'

'At first glance, I would agree, but smell and taste it.'

The Sargent sniffed it.

'It smells like ash.'

The Captain gave a nod. The Sargent then licked the substance and then spat it out.

'Recognise the taste?' asked the Captain.

'Yes, it's the same taste that I get when I fire a pistol. It tastes of gunpowder!'

'Very good Sargent. So what can we surmise from this fact?'

'That gunpowder was used to seal up the cave!'

'Exactly. The Piper knew we would follow and knew we would try to get through. So he made sure we couldn't!'

'So how are we going to get through?' asked the Sargent.

'We're not. Again it's a ruse. I believe that there is another way down which we are yet to find.'

'It'll be like trying to find a needle in a haystack.'

'I agree. I think another chat with our ginger-haired friend may be needed. If you can handle that Carruthers. See if he knows anything that may help us in the search. Offer an incentive if needed. I would join you but I have another interview to carry out.'

***

Molly sat in the Mayor's office in Gunne House. The Mayor, Lord Mulberry, sat opposite her with Captain Campion on his right and Reverend Nicholas on his left. The room was small and felt cramped with the three men sitting opposite her. The Reverend made her feel uncomfortable. She could see his eyes looking up and down her bodice like she was a piece of meat. He couldn't keep his eyes off her bosom, and so Molly pulled her cloak around herself to cover her bust.

'Tell us what happened again,' said Lord Mulberry.

'How many times am I going to tell the same story? I've told you three times today already and nothing new has come to mind!' she replied.

'You'll do as you are told young Lady!' said the Reverend now angry that his view had been obscured by her cloak.

'What the Reverend is meaning,' said Lord Mulberry. 'Is that we need your help. We need to make sure nothing is missed.'

'Gentlemen, if I may,' said the Captain.

The two other men remained quiet.

'After you alerted us to the disappearance of the children, how did you know where to go?' he asked.

'It was when that chap came and said that he saw the Piper heading South. You and the others chased after them but the chap started acting suspiciously. He started running the opposite way heading toward the Brading Downs. I decided to follow him. He was a fast runner and I struggled to keep up but I kept going and eventually found the place.'

'Thank you, Miss. You also told us of the altercation at the cave, and how the cave collapsed. Tell me miss, when the cave collapsed, was there an explosion from the cave?'

'Yes, there was definitely an explosion!' said Molly. 'Actually, thinking about it, there were two explosions. One small muffled one before the cave collapsed and then a large one immediately after.'

'Did you get hit by any of the debris or did it simply collapse straight down?'

'No, I got hit by quite a few stones and rocks.'

'Interesting. Can I ask about the altercation? What happened exactly?'

'The Piper and Thomas were arguing, but I didn't hear anything that was said as I had just arrived. When I got there they had finished arguing, and I saw the Piper head into the cave followed shortly by Thomas.'

'Did either of them assault the other?'

'No,' she replied.

'So where did the blood come from?'

'Err, Thomas got, um, struck from a falling rock.'

'I'm sorry Miss, but the amount of blood that was on the floor came from more than just a rock. Tell us the truth.'

'Thomas accidentally got shot.'

'By a pistol?'

'Yes.'

'Who fired it?'

'It was an accident, I swear! It just exploded!'

'Who fired it, Miss?'

'Me!'

Molly began to cry.

'It's no use crying!' said the Reverend.

The Captain raised his hand to stop the reverend from speaking.

'She obviously killed the lad!' said the Reverend ignoring the Captain.

'No Reverend,' replied the Captain. 'There was a trail of blood leading into the cave. Obviously, the lad walked in! Molly, may I call you Molly?

Molly nodded.

'Molly,' continued the Captain. 'Where did the pistol come from?'

'Thomas' sister gave it to me. I don't know where she got it!'

'What happened to it after it exploded?'

'I dropped it on the ground. I was in shock about Thomas.'

'Was a pistol found?' said the Captain to the Mayor.

'No,' replied Lord Mulberry. 'My guards never reported it. I'll have them check the area again.'

The discussion was interrupted by the ringing of a bell. It was coming from the lockup.

CHAPTER 9

THOMAS & JOHN

Thomas sat on his sleeping pallet in the stone room thinking. His attempts at trying to loosen the shackles around his ankles were useless. A candle flickered in a far corner out of reach, and a cup of water sat on the table where he and the Piper had talked.

I need to get out of here and save the others, but how? he thought to himself. *John appeared close to death and Lucy looked dreadful too.*

The thought of them both made his eyes well up.

I should have been more careful walking into this rat's nest!

Thomas looked about the cell and could see nothing that could help him. There wasn't even a loose stone where he could attempt to smash the chains or shackles. The candle was too far away and probably wouldn't be of any use anyway. The cup of water was there but he could not think what to do with it that would help him escape. Thomas wished that he still had the flintlock with him, but the Piper must have taken it after capturing him. He could have attempted to break the lock with it. There was only one logical thing to do but he didn't like it.

It'll never work! The Piper is smart! He'll work it out quickly but I do need to try something! I can't just sit here and do nothing!

So Thomas sat waiting for the Piper to return, and hoped he wouldn't have to wait long.

***

Lucy had seemed more distant over the next few days since her chat with John about her daydreaming. He'd been worrying about her more and more ever since. She had told John that she hadn't eaten or drank for a few days, and that worried him even more. John had even seen her avoiding the food and water in the garden, even when others insisted that she partake of it. John was also worried about her strange behaviour. She had mentioned a few more situations where she felt displaced. They seemed to be more frequent and more intense, but still, she refused to eat or drink. John had tried several times to encourage her, but she dismissed him every time.

John became so worried about her that he decided to talk to the Piper about it. If anyone knew what was happening then it would be him, and so John began to search the garden in order to find him.

After several hours of searching without success, John decided to head to the large wooden building on the hill. The same building where the Piper had spoken to the children when they had first arrived. He walked up the wooden steps to the porch of the building and pushed open the double doors. The room was empty. Even the chairs and benches that were first there were now gone. The room was completely bare. John found it strange but just presumed that the Piper had moved it all out.

John began to look around the outside of the building. There was no sign of the Piper anywhere. John decided to try one more place before he gave up looking for him. He thought the Piper might be at the forbidden tree. John walked for some time in order to reach the tree but as he approached he saw that the Piper was not there. He was about to head off to see his friends, Will and Alice, when John suddenly heard a strange cutting noise. Immediately he thought that someone was working nearby so decided to take a look.

He followed the noise which led him near the strange tree and the river that flowed past. He found a path that had been cut into the brambles near the riverbank and so followed the path. The path was only around ten yards long, and at the end he found Lucy working.

'Lucy? What are you doing here?'

'I'm working!' she replied firmly, not sounding herself.

Lucy carried on working with her tools, cutting the brambles and trying to make a path.

'Lucy, I'm worried about you! You haven't been yourself for days.'

Lucy stopped working and turned to her brother. Despite working hard, she still looked neat and clean though tears stained her face.

'Something is wrong with this place John!'

'You've said it a million times!'

'I know, but let me show you something strange!'

Lucy reached into a gap in the brambles and began to pull out a long thick branch. When the branch had been fully retracted John saw that the end was on fire.

'Are you crazy! Shouted John grabbing the branch. 'Do you want to burn the whole garden down!'

'The brambles won't burn!'

'What do you mean they won't burn?'

'Try it yourself!' she replied.

John held the flame on the branch close to one of the brambles. Nothing happened. John then moved the branch away and touched the bramble. It wasn't even warm. The fire seemed to have no effect.

'See!' said Lucy.

That's strange! thought John. *I've never seen anything like it.*

'Maybe it's some sort of protection!' said John unconvincingly. 'The garden is supposed to keep us safe. It would be a pretty poor garden if you could easily burn it to the ground!'

'It's no good showing you anything!' she replied.

Lucy then threw her hands in the air and stormed off. John remained a moment trying to understand. It was strange, but John's theory must be right.

Another question to ask the Piper, he thought. *If I could actually find him!*

CHAPTER 10

THE PIPER & LUCY

The Piper sat at his desk in his study. A candle flickered casting light across the table, and the book in front of him. The book was covered in words, pictures, and diagrams. He replaced his easel into its inkwell and sat back. A rat scurried across the table near the book almost knocking his flagon of ale all over it.

'Get away!' shouted the Piper. 'You'll spoil my work.'

He hit the rat hard, causing it to fall to the ground. It scurried out the open door squeaking as it went.

The Piper closed his book and tossed it onto a pile in a nearby corner. He then looked over one of the maps that were laid out in front of him. He picked up his easel and drew a cross at one of the tunnels.

That's the Brading Downs tunnel closed off. he thought to himself. *I need to explore the next one. I wonder where it will take me!*

The Piper drew a circle around another part of the map.

I'll try here next. he thought.

He stood from his chair and gulped down the last of the ale from his flagon.

Now to pay a visit to Mr Wolf. I'll get him to take care of a certain beautiful young lady for me. He owes me a favour, so I'm sure it'll be fine. The kids are all tucked up nicely in my land of wonder and the lad is securely locked away. My babies will keep watch.

The Piper donned his hat and coat and then left the room closing the door behind him.

***

Lucy woke up. Her head hurt and her throat was dry. Her eyes also hurt from the light shining close to her face. She turned over away from the light and tried to get her bearings.

She had gone to sleep in the grove of trees next to John, as she had done every night in the garden since she arrived. She remembered thinking that evening as she went to sleep that her hallucinations had gotten worse. She worried that she might not even wake up the next morning. Lucy had however woken up, but not in the grove of trees in the garden.

She had woken up in a very large room that was filled with beds. She felt aches and sores all over her body, especially her feet and back. She reached down to her ankles wanting to rub her pain away but felt the cold metal of shackles around them. Lucy began to panic and tried to pull on them. They would not budge no matter how much she pulled. It was as she was trying to remove the shackles that she felt an object digging into her, no doubt the cause of her back pain. She reached around to grab the object that was causing the discomfort and felt the Piper's pistol. She still had it! She quickly tucked it away into her belt and looked about the room. She could see all the other children that she had arrived with. They too were each chained at their feet and were laying on a bed, but each of them appeared blissfully unaware of it. They were all in a deep sleep.

Behind her she sensed movement. Lucy slowly turned around and saw John laying on the bed next to her. He too had shackles around his ankles and he too seemed completely unaware of it.

John looked really bad. His clothing was ragged, ripped, and dirty, and they hung off his frail body. His face was withdrawn but he had a beaming smile and was mumbling to himself.

Lucy pulled herself out of the bed and crawled over to John.

'John! Wake up, John!' she cried out.

John didn't respond but carried on muttering to himself.

I have no idea where I was but I escaped! she thought to herself. *I need to somehow help John to escape!*

She began to shake him and shout at him but to no avail.

I need to try something else! she thought.

CHAPTER 11

JOHN & LUCY

John was walking with Will and Alice along the riverbank in the garden. It was another beautiful day with not a cloud in the sky. John was worried about Lucy again. He had woken that morning and she was gone. He was sure that she was fine, after all, they were in paradise. But there was not a sign of her anywhere.

He asked Will if he had seen her but he hadn't. It still amazed John that Will now had eyes and could see. John was so happy for him. Will loved it and he soaked in every new thing he saw.

Alice had said that she hadn't seen Lucy either. It was lovely hearing Alice talk, she had such a sweet voice. John especially loved it when Alice sang. She had a beautiful singing voice. The voice of an angel he had told her.

'I'm sure she's just gone on one of her explorations of the garden,' said Will.

'Will's right, she's always curious. I'm sure she's fine,' said Alice.

'I know you're both right, but I've just got a bad feeling about it!' replied John.

'In this place! You're being silly John. This place is wonderful!' said Alice.

'Precisely!' added Will.

'Stop it you two. You don't have to gang up on me,' laughed John.

The three walked on by the river and saw some of the other children playing in the water. The children were playing with a walrus and a dodo bird. The scene made them all smile.

Suddenly, John began to feel pain. It was his jaw and cheeks. They felt like they were on fire. Will and Alice saw that something was wrong.

'What's happened John?' said Alice. 'Are you ill?'

John grimaced.

'I don't know,' he replied.

Will put his hand on John's shoulder.

'Maybe, it's something you ate,' said Will.

John felt the pain again but this time more intense. His hands and fingers started to feel like pins and needles were sticking in them. He looked at his hands and saw they were dirty with mud and blood. Fresh scabs were scattered randomly on his hands too.

'Look at my hands? What's happening!' cried John.

'They look fine John,' said Will.

'There's nothing there,' said Alice.

John looked at Will and Alice and they were beginning to fade away. John looked around the garden and began panicking. Everything was disappearing.

John fell onto his back on the floor but instead of landing on grass, he landed on something hard. Everything then went black but he could hear Lucy's voice.

'John! Wake up! Wake up!'

John opened his eyes to see Lucy shouting at him and slapping his face.

'Lucy.....I'm awake!'

Lucy hugged him tight as John looked around the room. He suddenly felt weak and very afraid.

***

John was awake! Lucy began to cry with relief. His body felt very frail in her arms as she hugged him. He was also very dirty and stank of something too vile for words.

'Where are we?' he asked shakily.

'I don't know. I was hoping you might have some idea.'

'No, I don't.'

'How do you feel?'

'Sick. I feel very weak and my cheeks feel like someone's beaten me black and blue!'

'I'm sorry,' she said.

'Don't worry.'

He smiled at her. The smile gave Lucy hope and made her feel that they would be all right.

'I take it the garden place wasn't real!' he said. 'Some kind of dream I suppose.'

'I think so. I think the water we drank put us into that world. It was like a prison!'

'A prison you would never want to leave!'

'Exactly.' she replied.

'You were right about the Piper, Lucy!'

'We've got no time for I told you so. We need to get out of here. Do you feel strong enough to move?'

'Yes, I'll be fine.'

'We need to look at these chains that are holding our ankles. There's some kind of lock but I can't see it properly. You take a look.'

John moved so that he could see the lock.

'We need something to pick the lock with,' he said.

'There's nothing here!'

'Hang on a second! I think I have something,'

John reached into his pocket and felt the small knife that he used the day he was attacked by the rats.

'I have a knife,' said John.

'Try it!'

After using it to play around with the lock, the mechanism sprang open releasing Lucy.

'Thank you! Let me take a look at yours,' she said.

Lucy then examined John's lock with his knife in hand. It was more complicated than it looked, but after a few minutes of trial and error, she managed to open it.

'Come on,' she said. We need to get out of here!'

Lucy picked John up and carried him on her back. He felt lighter than the last time she had carried him.

'What about the other children?' he asked. 'We can't just leave them!'

'We have to John. Just for the moment. We need to get to safety before the Piper returns and notices we're missing. We'll come back for them later, I promise.'

'I understand. Let's get going.'

Lucy crept across the large room with John on her back. They reached the main door and surprisingly it opened.

CHAPTER 12

THOMAS & THE PIPER

Thomas sat on the floor feeling resigned. His plan had been to tell the Piper that he had changed his mind and to go along with what the Piper said. Then when he was released he would escape. The problem was, however, that the Piper hadn't returned since their last discussion. And so Thomas continued to sit waiting for the Piper to return.

Thomas used this time he had to think about Molly and his family and remember the good times they had.

He really missed Molly. He'd only known her a short time but it felt like he'd always known her. He loved her without question and knew she loved him back.

He thought about his poor mother and hoped that she did not suffer when she died. The thought caused him to well up. He thought about his innocent father and wondered if he would ever see him again.

And then he thought about Lucy and John. He loved them both so, so much. He thought of them back when they were all together as a family. He remembered John and Lucy laughing and playing together. He also remembered them both getting up to mischief. He could hear them talking in his mind. Talking about escaping this place. He then realised that the voices were not in his mind, he could actually hear them! Their voices were coming from the barred window in the door.

'Lucy! John! Are you here?'

He saw the two heads of his siblings through the small barred window.

'Thomas!' they called in unison.

The door opened and Lucy stepped into the room with John on her back.

Thomas began to cry. Seeing his brother and sister filled him with such relief, especially John whom he had feared was now dead. They both looked terrible and this upset Thomas. John looked like a bag of bones as Lucy put him on the floor in from of Thomas. John began to hug him while Lucy went to the shackles around his feet.

'I've missed you so much John!' said Thomas hugging him tightly.

'I've missed you too.'

John began to weep in his arms. The chains unlocked and Lucy tossed them aside. She then threw her arms around both Thomas and John.

'Thank you Lucy!' said Thomas.

He kissed his sibling's heads and the three held each other tight, neither of them wanting to let go. After a few minutes, Lucy spoke.

'There's no time for reunions. We need to get out of here!'

'Let's get moving,' replied Thomas.

He stood shakily and gained his balance. He felt weak but was ready to get moving. He picked up John and slung him onto his back.

'Just like old times,' said John.

'Really!' said Thomas. 'You been in a creepy dungeon before?'

John and Lucy laughed. It was the greatest sound Thomas had heard for a long time. The three left the cell and stepped into the corridor.

'The other children are here too,' said Lucy. 'We left them behind to get to safety and get help.'

'We'll come back as soon as we can.' replied Thomas.

'How will we know which way to go and how to get out of here?' said John.

'I'm not sure,' said Thomas. 'I guess we try the way we came.'

The three moved off ready to escape the building they were in and the cavern.

***

Another deed is done! he thought to himself smiling. *That girl is going to experience a lot of pain.*

The Piper brushed dirt from his coat and shoulders. He reached into his inside pocket and took out a cigar. He struck a match with his thumb, lit the cigar, and drew a deep puff on it. After a few more deep puffs, he looked around the large cavern. The lighthouse could vaguely be seen in the far distance, a few miles away.

It's a long walk but walking is good for the mind. That's probably why I enjoy it so much.

The Piper began the long walk back to the lighthouse. The Piper had just reached the outskirts of the area in the cavern that he called the village. He looked upon the village which was brightly lit by the lighthouse. The Piper pulled out his pocket watch and opened it up to check the time.

Another hour or so before everyone gets up, he thought. *I hope they're enjoying the garden but then again they'll love paradise even more.*

As the Piper walked he saw the door to the dormitory open.

They're up early today. That's strange. I can normally set my watch to the time they would normally be up.

The Piper saw the three figures emerge from the door. It was the girl Lucy in front and Thomas followed behind with John on his back.

'Halt!' shouted the Piper.

Matthew Ryan

The children saw him and ran toward the bridge.

Where are the flaming rats? he thought.

The Piper went to draw his pistol from the holster at his waist but it wasn't there.

Stupid man, I forgot to pick it up after throwing it on the ground!

The Piper started to run after them and pulled his pipe from his pocket. He then put the pipe to his lips and began to play his tune. His running made the task more difficult but the rats heard it and began pouring from their nests. The three children were now across the bridge. The Piper played a tune that caused the rats to chase them. The rats chased the children across the bridge and followed as they ran toward the lighthouse. The Piper reach the bridge and ran across trying to catch up. He then saw something had changed. Lucy had split from Thomas and John and it was only her heading toward the lighthouse. The rats all followed her. Thomas and John had gone the opposite way. The Piper decided to leave the rats to deal with Lucy. He would deal with Thomas and John himself.

CHAPTER 13

MR HOPPER & THE CAPTAIN

The guard fell to the ground as Hopper pulled the knife from his neck. Hopper had known the guard as Benjamin, they had attended school together as children. Hopper smiled as he watched his old school friend bleed to death.

Hopper had been in the lockup and had called out to Benjamin who was at his post outside the door. Hopper had asked Benjamin for a cup of water, for old time's sake. Benjamin had agreed. He brought in a cup of water and even talked to Hopper as he drank. Benjamin had got up to leave the lockup but despite his shackles Hopper had been on him in two steps. Hopper grabbed a knife that was in a sheaf on the guard's belt. He pulled the knife and held it at Benjamin's neck.

'Unlock my chains, then let's get moving!' said Hopper

The guard obeyed and unchained him. The two then began to walk out of the lockup and into a holding area below the Town Hall.

'It's no use, Hopper,' said the guard. 'There are two other doors to get through and I don't have a key.'

'I know that my old friend, but there are other ways to open locked doors!'

They carried on walking and headed toward a large bell.

'Do you remember what you used to call me at school?' asked Hopper.

'I can't remember!'

'You used to call me the gingerbread man! Why?'

'Honestly Hopper, I can't remember!'

'It was because I was ginger and the son of a baker.'

'That was a long time ago. We were kids!'

'Do you beg for forgiveness?'

'Yes, of course. I'm sorry Hopper, I truly am!'

Hopper drove the knife into the guard's neck.

'Apology accepted Benjamin!'

He pulled the knife out causing the body to slump to the ground. Hopper then stripped the body, swapped clothes, and then put the body back in the lockup in such a way that his face could not be seen. Hopper then returned to the bell and rang it hard so that the whole town would hear.

Ringing the bell will cause them to open the doors to come in. I'll then slip out without them noticing! he thought to himself.

He moved toward the exit door and pulled his hat down a little further to shadow his face. He heard the keys turn and the door opened. Two guards charged in.

'Quick!' shouted Hopper. 'I think he's killed himself!'

The guards ran off in the direction of the lockup. Hopper stepped through the two open doors. Other guards ran past him into the holding area. Hopper let them pass and then saw the coast was clear and so ran out of the Town Hall. He immediately dived into an alley but knew he had been seen.

'Halt!' shouted the Sargent, and another guard.

He ran down the alley as fast as he could.

Hopper jumped over a stone wall at the rear of the town hall. If he could make it to the stable across the field, a hundred yards away, he knew he could escape on a horse. He continued running through the long grass of the field.

He took a moment to glance back. The guard was some distance away but the Sargent was catching up. Hopper was impressed. He was fast, another reason why they called him the gingerbread man, but the Sargent was faster. The Sargent had almost caught up with him. He was twenty yards away from the stable and knew he wouldn't make it.

The Sargent grabbed him.

Hopper spun and drove the knife in his hand straight into the Sargent's chest. The Sargent slumped falling on top of him. Hopper pushed the body aside and got back to his feet. The other guard had caught up considerably in the scuffle. Hopper aimed and threw his knife. It hit the guard's leg causing him to stumble.

'Run, run, run, as fast as you can. You can't catch me, I'm the gingerbread man!'

Hopper ran off toward the stable leaving the guard crawling toward the Sargent who lay dying on the floor.

***

Today was the day that the Captain had always dreaded. He had always hoped that this day would never come but here it was. It was the day he had to bury someone that had been trained by him and served under him. It was true that Sargent Stephen Carruthers was a grown man and knew the dangers of the job, but the Captain viewed him as still under his care. Everyone who had ever served under him, who was trained by him, was always viewed by him as his responsibility. If they didn't do the job properly, or if they were injured, or worse killed, the Captain felt like he was at fault.

The Captain had fought in battles, and had worked as part of several police forces, and lost many companions. This though was different, those were fully trained men. Carruthers was not. The Captain felt responsible and it cut him deep to think of the pain he went through as he lay on the floor dying.

The graveyard was empty. No one had turned up for the service except the Reverend Nicholas, and he had left quickly afterward.

'I'm sorry Stephen.' The Captain said out loud to no one.

'I will make sure justice is carried out.'

The Captain laid a red rose across the place where the Sargent was buried. He took his pipe from his pocket, lit it, and smoked as he stood thinking of his friend. Sargent Carruthers was a good man, the Captain reflected. His view and opinion of the various crime scenes that they had investigated together had taught even the Captain many lessons. The Captain always looked outside the box but sometimes, as Carruthers had shown him, the answer was simply inside the box. The simplest answer was normally the right one. Yes, he was a good man, terrible with the ladies but a good man.

The Captain's thoughts were disturbed by the neighing of horses near the gate to the cemetery. The Captain looked back and saw a small group of individuals he hadn't seen in a long, long time. He walked over to them.

There were four horses of different colours. One white, one black, one pale, and one red. On the red horse sat a handsome man with blonde hair and a moustache to match. He was dressed finely and had a pistol strapped at his waist. On the black horse sat a beautiful woman with long red hair. She had a selection of daggers attached to various belts across her body. On the pale horse sat a man with black skin. He was covered in scars and had the face of a hunter. The white horse had no rider but was the most beautiful of the four horses. The woman spoke as the Captain approached.

'We were told you were here. We heard the news. Such a waste of a good officer!'

'I know.' replied the Captain. 'I'll miss him.'

'It's good to see you Cap!' said the man with blonde hair.

'It's good to see you too, all of you.'

The Captain walked over to the white horse and began to stroke it.

'And it's good to see you most of all!' said the Captain.

'Can you believe it?' said the man with the blonde hair laughing. 'We come all this way and the Cap is more interested in his horse than us!'

'Nothing's changed there!' said the woman with a smile on her face.

The black-skinned man rolled his eyes.

'It's so good to see you girl!' said the Captain as he mounted the horse.

'What's the job Captain?' asked the woman.

'We are going after the man that killed Stephen!'

'It's just like old times!' said the man with blonde hair. 'The four horsemen ride again!'

'I hate it when you call us that!' said the Captain.

The four rode off and out of the town of Brading with the Captain, on his white horse, leading the way.

CHAPTER 14

LUCY & THOMAS

Lucy fled up the stairs of the lighthouse with the rats in pursuit. She was determined not to let her fear get the better of her. She glanced back and saw the flood of rats pouring up the stairs behind her. It looked like water running over a dry riverbed but upward if such a thing were even possible. The rats were still several yards behind but Lucy was beginning to tire out. The stairs led up higher into the lighthouse.

Upon reaching the top Lucy saw a door in front of her. She opened the door, stepped in, and then slammed the door behind her. She backed further into the room knocking over a chair and bumping a table that had various objects and papers on top. She heard the rats squeaking as they reached the top of the stairs and the door. She grabbed a poker that was sitting next to a fireplace that had a fire burning in it. She braced herself ready for the rats to break in and attack.

The sweat on her forehead was beginning to run down her temples and her heart was beating so fast that she thought it might explode. She quickly glanced around the room to see if there was another exit, but there wasn't. She could still hear the rats squeaking but there was no sound of them trying to get through the door yet.

Lucy again looked about trying to find something better than the poker to fight the rats off with. The room was filled from top to bottom with books, piles, and piles of them. She saw a picture on one wall and a mirror on the other. Nothing of interest stood out to her until she looked at the table she had bumped into as she rushed into the room.

Lucy moved slowly to the table, keeping her weapon held high ready for the rats. As she approached the table, Lucy glanced at the contents scattered on top.

There was a burnt-out candle and an empty glass bottle. There were maps and also a writing stylus. Most intriguing of all was what sat on top of one of the maps. It was the Pipers powder flask and a small cluster of lead shots. Seeing the objects reminded Lucy of the pistol she had tucked into her belt. She had forgotten about it during her escape from the rats. Lucy threw the poker aside, pocketed the flask and shots, and pulled the weapon from her belt. She checked to see if it was loaded and pulled the hammer back ready to shoot. She stood for a moment with shaking hands, pointing the pistol at the door. Lucy suddenly realised that the squeaking had stopped.

Slowly, Lucy crept to the door and put her ear to it. Everything outside was deathly quiet.

Lucy's hands shook as she reached for the handle of the door. She gripped the handle and turned it slowly. Her heart thumped hard in her chest as she opened the door just a crack.

Nothing happened.

Lucy opened the door more. The rats were gone. She looked down the stairs to see the heaving mass of rats pouring down the same way they came. Lucy followed the fleeing rats.

***

Thomas had fled with John on his back, in the opposite direction to Lucy. He knew that the Piper would follow him hopefully allowing Lucy to get away. Thomas fled the opposite way from the Piper's lighthouse.

They hadn't planned their escape very well, but then again, they were not expecting to see the Piper so soon. He remembered shouting to Lucy to split up but now that they had done that he didn't know what to do. Thomas slowed down his run feeling tired. An idea then struck Thomas.

'I'm going to confront him, John!'

'He'll kill you!' John replied.

'Not if I can sneak up on him. Do you still have your knife?'

John rummaged around in his pocket and pulled the knife out. He then handed it to Thomas.

'The question is, how do we sneak up on him?' asked John.

'If we can make it back across the bridge to the buildings, we could ambush him there!'

'Good idea,' said John.

Thomas continued to run and circled back round heading toward the bridge again. The Piper was some distance away but was still in pursuit.

'He's catching up!' shouted John as Thomas ran.

'How far behind is he?'

'A hundred yards or so!'

Thomas ran faster and could feel the burning in his chest. He also felt the aching of his legs as he pushed to move faster. He focussed on the bridge and within a few moments was bounding across it. The bridge shook and swayed as Thomas crossed with John on his back.

'It's all over Thomas.' shouted the Piper.

Thomas reached the other side and immediately stopped and turned to face the Piper who had just reached the foot of the wooden bridge. The Piper looked fine despite his running. He wasn't panting for breath like Thomas was and the Piper didn't even appear to have broken a sweat.

The Piper

'It's over! There is no escape from wonderland!' said the Piper.

'Wonderland? This place is hell on earth! You enslaved those children and you call it a wonderland. You're completely insane!'

'Insane? I'm a mastermind! I set everything up, all from the very beginning, to get to this very point.'

'What do you mean you set everything up?'

'I enslaved those rats with my pipe and have taught them how to act. After killing so many of them they soon learned to obey. I was the one who sent them into the town of Brading. I was the one who trained them to kill the townsfolk and the bull. I was the one in disguise as a rat catcher putting everything in place. I was the one who put a stone into the barrel of the pistol that exploded next to your head. I was the one who nursed you back to health to take over. I am the one who has saved those children from a life of nothing and gave them a chance of everlasting life in paradise on earth! That's not insanity, that's pure brilliance!'

'Those children were going to have to die first! You were going to kill them!'

'It was all in the lord's name. They would die but would awaken in paradise, just as the good book says. I may be condemned for doing so but at least they would be saved!'

'You killed our mother!' shouted Thomas.

'I'm sorry Thomas but I didn't! It wasn't me, it was your father!'

'No,' said Thomas. 'I don't believe you!'

'I know it's a bit of a plot twist but it's true! I have no reason to lie!'

Thomas looked about in disbelief hoping a way to escape would present itself.

CHAPTER 15

THE PIPER & JOHN

The Piper was beginning to lose his temper with Thomas. He had given the lad enough chances to listen to him but the boy stubbornly refused.

'I'm finished with you, Thomas! I hoped you would help me save the children, and others too. I hoped that you would carry on this important work!' said the Piper.

'I'm sorry to be a disappointment!' Thomas replied.

'Don't be sorry Thomas! I truly thank you!'

'For what?'

'For showing me that you were not the one. As a thank you I'm going to do something for you!'

'And what's that?' asked Thomas.

'I'm going to kill you!'

He could see the look of fear on Thomas and John's faces and it made him smile. The Piper reached into his pocket for his pipe and began to play it.

The Piper saw Thomas look around as thousands upon thousands of rats poured out of every hole and every nook. The rats surrounded Thomas and John on their side of the river while the other rats, most of whom had ran from the lighthouse, stood behind the Piper on his side.

The Piper

'Any last words?' asked the Piper.

'Just a question. How can you control the rats without your pipe?'

'I can't, but as you clearly see I do have my pipe!'

'That's very interesting!' said a girl's voice from behind.

The girl Lucy was standing directly behind him aiming his pistol at him. The Piper didn't realise the pistol had been fired until he felt the pain. The crack of the pistol echoed in the large cavern, but it was his hand that had drawn his attention. The hand that had been holding the pipe. A large portion of his hand was missing and the pipe lay broken on the floor.

Lucy stepped away and ran to Thomas and John across the bridge as the Piper fell to his knees trying to nurse his ruined hand. Blood seeped through his fingers as he tried to put pressure on the wound with his good hand. The Piper stood and looked at the three children with fire in his eyes.

'You'll pay for that! All of you!' screamed the Piper.

He strode toward the bridge furious. Thomas gave Lucy John and prepared to fight the Piper. He held the knife ready outstretched. The Piper smiled as he saw Thomas stand in position ready to fight.

'You're a fighter, I'll give you that Thomas! I hope Molly puts up as much of a fight when the wolf comes for her!'

'What did you say?' said Thomas looking dumbfounded.

'You heard me! The wolf is going to see your beloved!'

'You liar!'

The Piper saw Thomas was beginning to look agitated and so used the opportunity to pounce. The Piper ran at Thomas with a look of pure hatred on his face. He was almost upon him and could hear his siblings calling his name, but then something happened that truly shocked him. A rat bit his leg. He looked down to see the rat gripped onto him and saw blood coming from the wound. He slapped the rat away, and then another rat bit his hand. Another then jumped at his other leg and began biting. Then another attacked, and another. The rats were beginning to swarm the Piper on the bridge. The Piper thrashed about and screamed in pain as more and more rats joined in the attack.

***

John watched as the rats drove the Piper over the edge of the bridge and into the river. The rats all jumped in after him biting and scratching him. The scream from the mouth of the Piper was like that of an unknown creature. The high-pitched wail sent shivers up John's spine. As the swarm of rats devoured the Piper, the water of the river began to turn to blood.

John wanted to look away in fear but knew he had to watch. The Piper had manipulated him so much that he needed to watch him die. And die he did. He died by the same hand that he used to kill others.

Poetic justice! thought John.

After the Piper and the last of the rats floated away, Thomas swept him and Lucy up into his arms. The three hugged each other deeply and sat upon the ground next to the river.

'Thank you for saving us Sis!' said Thomas.

Lucy hugged them both tighter.

'It's over!' she replied.

'Do you think it was true what he said about Molly? Said Thomas.

'No,' replied John. 'He was a liar!'

'I hope you're right!' said Thomas.

They all let go of each other and all looked at the now quietly flowing river.

'And so ends the ballad of Sir Timerus the Piper!' said Thomas. 'He was as insane as he was cunning. He will not be missed!'

'What do we do now?' asked John.

'We need to free the other children and get out of here!' replied Thomas. 'I need to get back to Molly! I need to know she is safe!'

'But how can we escape this place? It's like a maze,' said John.

'I found maps in the Piper's study. Maybe they can help us escape.' said Lucy.

'Let's take a look,' said Thomas.

Lucy took the lead and walked them back toward the lighthouse picking up the broken pieces of the Piper's pipe as she went. Thomas followed closely behind with John now sitting on his hip as he walked.

For the next few weeks, the three worked hard to escape the Piper's nest. Thomas used the maps Lucy had shown him to plan a route out. In one of the Piper's many diaries, he talked about the island being inescapable. Like the island itself was some kind of prison. The ancient maps seemed to show routes that led to various locations on and off the island and even under the sea to unknown destinations. Thomas focussed on just finding a route back home.

Lucy was also hard at work too. She prepared some of the rundown houses in the cavern for the children who awoke. She also prepared food and drink for them, and for the journey, Thomas had told them that they needed to make.

John too was busy and was given one of the most important tasks. John woke the children and helped nurse them back to health. It took many days to save each child and some even longer. John's friends, Will and Alice, had taken weeks. Will did not want to return to a world where he was blind, and Alice thought of nothing more wonderful than the place she called wonderland. In time, the two awoke but they missed that special place.

After several more weeks, they were all finally ready to leave. Thomas stood at the entrance to a small cave with John on his back and with Lucy next to him.

'Do you think the Piper was telling the truth about Pa killing Ma?' asked John.

'No,' replied Thomas. 'The Piper was a liar and a cheat. We should never have trusted him from the start. Come on, let's go home!'

John and Lucy smiled at him as he led the way. John looked back to see the children following closely behind as they all entered the cave.

EPILOGUE

MOLLY

It was a cold autumn evening up on the Brading Downs. The leaves of most of the trees were beginning to turn the colour of toffee but a few held on to their green for as long as they could. A cold wind whipped up the red hooded cloak that Molly had wrapped around her. The sun had just begun to set and Molly knew that it would soon be time to head home.

So much had changed since the disappearance of the children of Brading. The fire from the night of the kidnapping destroyed many buildings and livelihoods. The criminal, now known as the Gingerbread Man, had escaped the town lockup killing a guard and also the Sargent from London. Shortly after, others arrived from the mainland to help hunt him down.

The ruling men over the island, the Brothers, had dispatched one of the Sisters to take control of the town and to begin rebuilding. The Sister was determined to get the town up and running again. The first thing the Sister did as soon as she arrived was to kill the Mayor, Lord Mulberry, and also Reverend Nicholas. Their bodies still hung now, a month later, in the town square as a reminder of who was in charge. No one dared to stand against one of the Sisters and so everyone cooperated and began to rebuild and resume their lives.

Not Molly though. Every day, since she had been found, Molly had packed a picnic basket with food and water and had headed back to where the cave had been. She normally arrived late morning and always travelled home at sunset. Every day she waited for her beloved Thomas to return to her. It had been six weeks since she first began to wait for Thomas and each day she became more desperate and depressed.

On this particular day, when the sun had set, Molly began to get ready to leave. As Molly gathered her things she heard a strange noise coming from a thicket behind her. She glanced back at the thicket but saw nothing. She presumed that it was a rabbit, or maybe a badger, and paid it no further attention.

As Molly began to walk away, she did not see the figure in the shadows. She didn't hear the individual creep up behind her, and she didn't expect to be grabbed from behind.

All those things happened in a blink of an eye, and Molly did not see it coming.

TO BE CONTINUED

Matthew Ryan

Printed in Great Britain
by Amazon

15380640R00150